THIS
EVERY
NIGHT

PATRICK MOORE

D1570670

AMETHYST PRESS
NEW YORK, NEW YORK

AN AMETHYST PRESS FIRST EDITION
COPYRIGHT © 1990 by PATRICK MOORE

Published in the United States of America by Amethyst Press, Inc., 462 Broadway, Suite 4000, New York, NY 10013.

COVER ART BY RUSS CLOWER
AUTHOR PHOTO BY ANNA LEVINE THOMPSON

Library of Congress Cataloging-in-Publication Data

Moore, Patrick, 1962-
    This every night / by Patrick Moore. — 1st ed.
        p. cm.
    ISBN 0-927200-06-6 : $8.95
    I. Title.
PS3563.O6265T4 1990
813'.54—dc20   90-43090
                                                    CIP

For Dino

With Special Thanks To Stan Leventhal, Ira Silverberg, Anna and David Thomson and ACT UP.

MONDAY

I must continually degrade myself. And to that end, as each evening fades to black from the city's natural steel gray, I go to walk, to face the night and its many pleasures. I gravitate to the western edge of an island I live upon that is only occasionally recognized as an island. There is a rigid grid stretching across Manhattan that begins to dissolve only as one moves west through the Village and it is in that direction that I move this night, this every night. For on those thin strips of broken concrete that border the edge of this island, one becomes aware of an unseen constant in this geography, the water surrounding my little world. Water seen only truly at night as it blackens and hides its true self, full of human waste. A sickly streaked blue gone in the late hours and replaced rather with a dark mystery rasping softly at the city's edges. It is towards those waters that I must always make my way as the sky darkens. For that liquid laps round the world connecting continent to state and wasteland to cityscape, pulling at the waste of our lives, distilling it into a human constant of degradation. And it is only through scale that degradation may attain greatness, only through connecting my poor heart to every other that my shame transfigures into the glory of my culture.

This evening is like every other both in its intent and appearance as I pass through my door with Franky holding it weakly open but avoiding my eyes at all cost. And I wonder what it is that he avoids in my eyes that I welcome from his aging face with its drooping black moustache and graceful Latino neck melting into a middle-aged man as it drops to a Santa stomach. Franky is one of the many people I know who refuse to be consistent in their dealings with me and therefore fill every moment with a nervous wait for their next slight and my next resentment. Tomorrow he will say hello and make some polite comment but tonight I am judged inadequate and do not exist. Why should I desperately seek the face of this man forty years older and from a different life? Franky's position on my long and variable list of grudges has risen.

Franky, like many people who slightly detest me, has become something of an obsession for me. I've decided to find out everything I can about this little man slumped against a great brass door, sort through every piece of trivial information I might garner from the other doormen until I determine what it is in me that repels him. There are five men who work in the building who have proven useful in the quest for Franky tidbits. The basic outline of his life was easy; lives in Queens, moved from the Dominican Republic thirty or forty years ago, married, divorced, one child, one male child. This list of facts tells me nothing, however. Nothing about Franky who hates me. Nothing about Franky whose shoulders creep up slightly as my coat brushes his hand, on purpose. The best details so far have come from Eddy, the late, late shift doorman who sits with me and eats his chips as the sun comes up and I've returned home, too tired now to finish the trip upstairs. Eddy has actually visited the house of Franky, and it is a house, an entire house, not an apartment. He describes the house as nearly bare of furniture and blindingly clean. White, bare walls. Did he visit all of the rooms or just the living room, I wanted to know. Eddy is a bit vague on this but does say he went to the second floor to use the bathroom and saw several rooms which were entirely empty. The bedroom was not empty, he says. What does he mean, not empty, I ask. Full, he teases, almost entirely full. What do you mean, Eddy, what exactly do you mean by full? Full, he chuckles, full to the brim. When Eddy has finished talking, he's finished talking and his great fuzzy black head rolls down on his fat neck as his toe traces the design of the floor. So it is that tonight as I peer at Franky's moustache and his white teeth, I think of fullness, of a room stuffed with something, a room overflowing with someone. He's got my attention, this man, simply by hating me.

One of New York's many sorrowful little parks borders my nightly path and I avoid looking at the florescent lights that illuminate its petrified trees and concrete paths. Rather its shadows draw and frighten me because I know that parks are holy places where much violence and beauty occurs and reoccurs. And the whispered call of "sense, sense" draws me on as I see men that I will never know and who are my enemies even as I desire them, because I desire them. I desire them because they are my enemies and rule a place holy to my culture, ensuring a dynamic of hate and adoration that draws us to these small forests. Men that hate me border every dirty park in this city, and therefore I dress like them with leather bunching around my shoulders and a baseball hat drawn backwards. Their hate dictates a beauty I avenge by imitating it, making it mine and a sexual object, something they dread and secretly hope for. All this park offers is a place for my thoughts as I pass westerly, steadily, and the hate of these men trembles next to the complete rage I feel towards them.

Parks, as I say, are almost always sacred and otherworldly at night. Some, however, attain a stillness that makes them truly noted among men around the world. Washington Square Park is not high in this hierarchy of public spaces. Not an equal, shall we say, to the overgrown, rat infested passion of the Circus Maximus or the winding paths of Athens' Public Gardens or even the repressed shrubs of America's great suburban green. This small patch of green surrounded by steel has been covered almost entirely in concrete and asphalt, leaving only a few trees to carry on the task of coloration. Police cars roll across the concrete paths constantly, for this is a park for the police, not the people. This is a park designed as a street so that cars may move easily while people feel exposed and soft against all the hardness of this public place. Perhaps even the rats were suddenly covered in concrete one day as I never see them anymore, only signs warning dog owners of the presence of poison for these concrete rats that no longer move but smell the lure of poison drifting through layers of earth and stone. This park is the La Brea Tar Pit of New York and I'm sure that not only animals lie crushed under the oppressiveness of the square, but human souls also crushed by the hate of this city, hate which manifests itself in starvation and disease and a disaster mentality reflected by the continuing party, the manic celebration of all we do not have as a community, the party that is sharp and manic and joyless. This is New York City in 1989 as the party continues.

The boredom of walking in Manhattan lies in traversing a grid that necessarily draws one always on the same route no matter the destination. Or perhaps it's the fact that the destinations are usually similar, if not indeed the same. Yet I live in a part of this city where legends have lived and a new heat is beginning to burn. So even though my conscious mind wonders if the diagonal to Seventh Avenue might prove more interesting, a primal part knows that America might tremble at the thoughts that occur in my people here in the West Village. It is here that the middle class becomes irrevocably politicized and in that plots the death of all it once loved. It is here that white boys sometimes talk of meeting others oppressed to join with them. It is here that each night rituals take place that ancient people could understand more fully than the woman that gave birth to me.

Even as our political makeup changes, obsessions remain constant and indeed may intensify as they are denied. Yes, I still look to the face of every man I pass and mcet the eyes of many on this search that is not confined to the dark now, this search that occupies each waking and sleeping and dreaming moment. And while I traverse Seventh Avenue into the true heart of this small area I note that I can even avoid traffic while cruising. Yellow taxis swerve narrowly past me as I have brief encounters with three men during the course of moving through the stream of cars. Each man is dissimilar in terms of clothing: one with a white tanktop, leather jacket and faded jeans; one with an outfit all in denim; and one in a suit which fits tightly around his ass. But all three share the same eyes, the eyes that I share which identify me and make me available to the pack. Mr. Denim turns to look, as do I, but now being on opposite sides of the Avenue the encounter seems overly complicated with no clear destination for protection of what promises to be a lengthy evening with names exchanged, probably false, and tortured small talk. Far wiser to continue to acknowledged locations made for this purpose and these locations lie beyond the end of Christopher Street with its endless boutiques of clothes best worn only to the health club. One of the most questionable has selected turquoise as the color of choice this season and although the snow has only recently left, each garment is made of the sheerest cotton and tailored for bicycle messengers.

This warming trend reflected in fashion unfortunately bodes of spring, a season trumpeted each year as a time of joy. The faces on Christopher are vaguely flushed by the warmth that I do not feel from a sun which should give warmth but does not yet. Shining down through the cold, the sun and this season remind me only of death, of snow melting to reveal what has rotted beneath through these long months of ice. Spring is the time of despair for all that know night and live there. What joy in the lengthening daylight of cold hours wrapped in wool, alternately repressive and comforting? I know the heat of summer will bring a much needed anger to this city but its arrival is still far off. Last summer's riots seemed to change something but only for a moment and enemies who should be allies remained enemies and the stupid rivalries of the Left returned all too soon. So what about riots, so what if New York shot its load one more time and then got bored again?

The bars that line Christopher have never been my favorites. They are overly social and the constant chatter only prevents what is really on our minds. I don't want to know you and your family and that dear friend sure to be famous soon. I don't want to know about our likenesses in taste and that glamourous night at the club and a brush with danger. I don't want to know anything about you, not your name, not even the sound of your voice. I do want to know the taste of your chest and the anonymous thrust of your cock. I do want to suck on your mouth to shut, to shut, to shut you up before you become less of a stranger, before your body falls away from knowing you.

These bars are from a time before I came to this city. This street is the street of a community which never existed for me. My community is not social but a necessity and exists only in the anonymity and rage of industrial buildings and empty streets and alleys never meant for the human trade. That's why this street is one I always walk, but on my way to somewhere else and these brothers are recognizable but not by name. This street is from another time when people were happy and stupid and believed they'd earned respect from the rest of this country. Now we know that this street is part of a town, which is part of a nation which is one large battlefield. Now we know that this street's power has passed.

The faces change shade as I progress west from white to a cultivated brown to a real brown and finally to black as I reach a large highway that separates the city from the waterfront. This highway, called a street but with nine lanes surely a highway, is nearly impossible to cross and I think that it may be on purpose. Not that the traffic signals flash "walk" too briefly so that pedestrians can be hit, but as a protection keeping all but the initiated from reaching the piers. One must bolt across without attention to the signal to reach the other side where cars circle incessantly. Most of the faces that bolt across are black but nearly all of the faces in the cars shine white.

The Piers is how this stretch is known but the focus is no longer on the rotting wooden arms extending into the river. They form only a backdrop to the real action of men and boys in cars and looking into cars and looking away as they sit on the concrete barrier and hear not the lapping of the water but the roar of engines and quieter sounds which are not really heard but felt by all here. The water is so basic to this situation that it is ignored as air is ignored by those who breathe it. The water and the filth that float in it are seldom examined but as I glance to it I see that it is alive. The splintered timber, human waste and consumer waste all caress the occasional face that floats among them, staring up at the grandeur of Manhattan. Those faces are of children that live here within sight of the Statue of Liberty, within sight of the World Trade Center, within sight of crumbling buildings and sanitation trucks that rumble past. Those faces are the same faces that are alive on the children that line the piers and are reflected in tinted glass. These are my brothers and sisters and our affinity is so great that we need never speak.

Lights in this city always shudder as they illuminate. The lights scattered down the length of the highway are meant to beautify this promenade, as if we didn't want it ugly, as if we'd come for a pretty little walk. And the harsh, harsh bulbs are shuddering tonight in their sockets, hidden by the globes favored by planners ten years ago, globes which were office marble international style white once but have now yellowed so far that they'll never come clean. The strollers are toplit in the distance, now that I look back, so that a long, straight shadow like a veil starts at their foreheads and drapes down to the feet. I'm glad to be on the other side now, away from those dreary little figures wandering home with their groceries and their video rentals and all the trappings of a normal life which seem so ridiculous here.

This concrete ledge that I lean upon, with my long leather coat pushed back to reveal my crotch, is slightly damp and cold even in summer and this evening it reminds me that many of the places I must go are damp and uncomfortable. The cars that pass never stop for the white boys, assuming that they are above the trade of bodies and a more formal approach must be made. An irritating assumption above its racism in that it eliminates many of the men and cars I find most desirable. The Lincolns with New Jersey license plates often yield the real beauties with overly short hair and white, white marble skin shadowed by beards or mustaches and bodies that are thick with muscle but slim at the same time as their smooth stomachs rumble down to hairy, black crotches and up to deep armpits. Only dark hair and bad accents can really do it, set me off so that a popper gets shoved up my nose and my face gets buried between fleshy man tits for hours on end. I wait for those men which I would never talk to and I wait for them and we will not talk but in barked commands and harsh whispers.

So it is tonight as the sky loses its last light and the unnatural glow of building lights replaces it, that I am excited by the fine selection offered on The Piers. Car after car glides by and the driver's head swings around to me, dark square heads and shoulders that indicate better things below. Now the car will never pull over and stop immediately beside me no matter how interested the driver because the ritual would be broken by the suddenness. Rather I must follow the car with my eyes and then on foot to where it has parked with its engine still purring. Then a slow, casual saunter past to show my goods and to look over the occupant as best I can in the dim light from the dashboard. This is when the difficulty of defining roles sometimes snuffs out the whole encounter before skin meets skin. Either play the hustler or establish one is just looking for sex, look tough or wet one's lips, it's incredibly complex.

What do they do in New Jersey to breed these beasts of men, these brainless beauties of macho-dom? Makes me hard to think of them. Someday I'll go to the big mall in Paramus and make a date with one of these guys. I want a short, packed one coming out of one of those fake wood paneling hair salons. That'll be my guy with the worst haircut in town, real short and blown up in front and with a fringe in back, oh, he'll practically bust out of those acid-washed jeans and that polo shirt when he sees me, waiting for my man, oh my mall man. Because I belong to him and his stupid talk about football and his real estate salesman job and his hatred of foreign food and his family in the same town and his chunking vowels and

17

his shiny new Corvette. My mall man will take me to Houlihan's for dinner because he loves those potato skins with cheddar and bacon bits and while I watch him chow down on those skins, I'll slip under the table and clean his already clean fat balls and suck his long, skinny dick and reach my hand up to feel the bulge of gym muscles under his skin. He'll feed me under the table, my mall man.

Finally, one that looks worth it comes back from the far end of the circular route for another pass by. The skin of the face is so white as to make it seem specially lit by a small spotlight and is topped by dark hair that is at once overly groomed and completely macho. Beyond that it's hard to tell much except that the man is probably around thirty and has a white shirt on. His glance lingers and the drive to a parking spot is relatively short. As I reach his window I slow to look down into the car and see his hand compulsively working the crotch of a business suit, his jacket thrown between the seats. He keeps nodding, little jerky nods and then looks back to his crotch covered by the grey, wrinkled fabric and massaged by one hand while the other one wanders mindlessly over the radio dial, switching stations.

Long stare and this I like best, when all are attractive. Men all attractive in their stares that imply hate and violence and long memories from below when men were glimpses caught in TV commercials of a hairy chest and an impossible bloated arm and not men but images of men. Still now an image when I look to eyes before touching when not touching yet but staring to their hate, to their deep reproach of me, of us, of what we're about to do and I say don't touch me but look through tinted glass and then we're back at that beginning time. It's before the touch that I feel the hate best and the hate is not mine but from outside and the hate not ours but from outside and we are given this hate to fetishize, we do not choose it. And now the stare is over and time to progress, time to go on to the act which defines all in these hours of darkness, in these hours when difference melts away by the river and my brothers come for the prowl.

Waves rustle the trash as I move beyond the car and circle, circle as the men do and I look to the water to reassure. I hear those waves at the edge of this island as I circle you and I know that men are doing this the world round, circling and waiting to touch one another in dark places, in shaded parks, in back alleys in the Mid East, in front of the newspaper walls in China, in the public toilets in Germany and in the parks world round as they listen to the gurgle of water from fountains and toilets and from pricks as the water goes. And then with my touch, the hand will go down on another crotch adding to the list, the list that says each time a man touches another man something is won and each time we add to that long list we throw off some of the hate, throw it in the fountain or the polluted river that borders whatever steel gray town we move through now. And I will touch and I will add to that list.

Now, now it comes that I am in and soft velour and

hard hand not known but gripping, gripping me now as my face turns skyward and the voice begins, "What else, what else do you like, tell me what else." Dark night by this river and your body stinks to me, smells not of what I came here for but of common sweat not cultivated but uncontrollable, sweat from a weak man. Cock hard, why hard now when I want to rush out when I grab for excuses and my cock hard as an intcrested boy but now you the boy and why now? "Shit on me. You like toilet men, let me clean out your ass." No, not right and not what I want why won't it shoot the nasty pudding and mine hard and yours limp when I'm the one not excited and the voice over and over and the voice spinning on, "What else do you like, what else, tell me what else." Your face was not with your body when I chose you and didn't choose you to be cruel, to be revolted, to want to end but in order to continue. No good, no good, no good and out, please out while I still can while I still can do this while I can continue this for the rest of the night when it doesn't come crashing down. "What else, what else do you like, tell me what else." I'm looking at my face in this glass and my mouth is pulling, ripping slowly at the corner and something is inside me with the repetition of this act no longer magic and killing me and not magic, not a time when I lift out of my body but when I watch blood starting to gush from me, from every orifice and I know that this act is killing me has killed me in a way that science does not know. My life is gone from that face in the window, young face but without the thing that drove it, drove it to walk hard streets and slam my body against others. A vital force taken from me by a virus that probably does not even exist in me, that may but from all signs does not yet in its absence has ripped the sex off of me with its metal claw. My mouth is pulling, pulling as the sound starts to shriek forth between a moan and the yelp of a dog stepped upon and just barely, just in time I pull the door handle. "What else, what else do you like, tell me what else."

Dear God, don't let me be losing this. Because I feel it leaving me now, how can it, but leaving, the urge to walk, to be in the night, the necessity of being always in the night and giving it hold over me. Something has changed inside of me that tears my sex away. It cannot be gone from my life because it defines me, every action of my life is defined in waiting for night to come and men to pass by me in the darkness and stop. Too soon. When not yet thirty it's too soon to lose one's sexuality without warning, with a simple change that was not heralded by a warning, a crisis, but has arrived and how can I live without that which defines me? Depression often follows me through my rituals and routines but never before a total revulsion, a boredom which is the most frightening because how could this life bore me? But it is another night wasted and I must admit that and accept that hours have passed in pursuit of what passes in minutes and then nothing, then alone and the famous camaraderie does not exist here, here I am alone as I have chosen to be while I wander the streets and clubs and filthy back rooms. People must have wasted their entire lives with the pursuit of this, each night moving from desolate space to desolate space in search of another cock and the nights are soon over as the waiting continues for just one or just one more. I know that people have given up their entire lives and plans to this and that it's a waste but I am now more afraid than I have ever been because I know that it has slipped away from me, my sex, my culture, my life and now I am so afraid because what will I do without it. What will I do tomorrow without my life?

TUESDAY

It's just that so much happens. To me. It's not that things haven't happened like this before but not with this frequency. And the difficulty is that they aren't climactic events but small, theatrical scenes that are dramatic but don't reveal anything to me, they don't add up and point to an avenue for change. Last night, for example. What does it mean that I should be addictively drawn to something and then repelled when I have it, unable to sink into the experience but left floating above it to witness my panic?

This evening I must be more careful in my choice of location and timing so that the proper build of events occurs. A later departure is called for, long past the sun has set and the lights of the Empire State Building dominate the view from my window. The waiting overshadows everything as eleven approaches and finally midnight is near. Only watching television, preferably MTV, is neutral enough that I can follow through with it. Song after song passes and I once again realize that I love MTV, that it is the only product of contemporary culture that is complete and enjoyable and looks good. The video I wait for is Metallica's new one, the one with the found footage from "Johnny Got His Gun." All over the country kids are looking at this and obsessing about violence and death and the beauty of it all as these biker types rip away at their electric guitars and the screen shows a man, a patient paralyzed on a table with a white box enclosing his face and the words come again, "Kill me, please God, let me die." That voiceover comes again and again as the guitars increase and millions of children that would hate me and beat me with their fists are joined with me looking at a screen and thinking of the beauty of it all. There may be hope in that moment when the spirit of Genet floats through a million television screens in this heterosexual nation and into the minds of psychotic youth.

I shower finally when I can bear the waiting no more. I use no soap but let the water clean my body so that it will smell only of itself with no other cloying scent. The water and my hands massage and abuse the hair that thickens between my tits and runs in a narrow column down the arc of my stomach and widens to the tangle around my cock. My legs are nearly bare of hair, as are my arms and my balls jut forward having been shaved bare to show their size. No erection comes as I scrub the pale skin, only an examination, an inventory, a taking account of the last few assets. The clothes are the same with the denim shirt and jeans and no underwear and the heavy black shoes topped by the long black leather of my coat. This is the costume I leave my building in every night as I go to walk.

The route this evening takes a quieter path, angling up away from the concrete of Washington Square and into the sedate tree lined blocks of the Village's most expensive areas. The quiet of these streets cutting at increasingly sharp angles is the prelude to a different kind of solitude at the end of my route. More and more brownstones drop away to be replaced by garages and buildings with anonymous facades. With the crossing of Eighth Avenue, there is an abrupt change of atmosphere as I enter the one area of this city that retains its character twenty-four hours a day and becomes harsher with every trendy restaurant or club that tries to capitalize upon it. Here asphalt again becomes cobblestones, limestone becomes brick and all surfaces are coated with the shiny smell of grease, fat and sweat as the city proudly lifts it skirts and reveals its filth.

The Meat District is a movie set where nothing real happens. These few blocks bordered by 14th Street on the north, the diagonal of Hudson Street on the east and the river on the west grow upward from Christopher finally taking form around Little West 12th. It is on Little West 12th Street that an enormous shadow is cast by a building that housed the epicenter of gay sexuality only a few years ago, a building now empty with warnings of unstable floors spray painted on the wall along with the misspelled epitaph of "Faggat." Thick chains loop again and again through the door handles, loops of metal to keep the devoted away, permanently. Surely the Mineshaft was the mutation of a whole culture into a mythical tribe that realized the power of ritual and induced insanity.

Each time I enter the Meat District it is by the path that will take me past the abandoned Mineshaft so that I can stop for a moment and smell and peer through the crack of a chained door into the past of everything I know. The blackness inside is complete but does not eradicate the memories of a room, a chapel with glowing white porcelain baptismal basins and Bach organ music mixed with the beat of disco echoing above. How can this be gone? Perhaps it isn't gone and never will be and only a building has emptied while the rage of our sexuality mounts again in these empty streets and while we no longer have a grand cathedral in which to worship we continue in small basements and back alleys and with every moment we continue what is uniquely ours, the gift that defines us and must never be lost. But as a tribute to a time that I was on the periphery of, I touch this building and I touch those that are gone through no fault of their own and I touch the life that they made for me and I will continue for them.

The stone of the building front is painted black and the smoothness of the paint is soothing as I linger on the corner looking at the furtive movements of men in leather and the arched backs of the drag queens working the street. Those queens are from the same family of gay children that cruised The Piers last night and every night. Where do they go finally when even this area has gone to sleep for a few hours before the meat workers arrive? Maybe they never sleep but roam continually until all the energy of their young bodies drains away, leaving them lifeless or mindless or finally going back to homes where they are despised by parents who are not really parents, not really those that love but only gave birth and not really parents but close torturers who own the rights to their children's bodies and use their love until it's time for the street. Time to send them to walk here through the greasy streets where chunks of white fat are left crushed under the square boots of straight men. Time to send them out to serve men that come from their wives and their buddies, men that take time out from fag bashing to get their dicks sucked by hungry little boys. I wish they were vampires and cannibals, those hookers, so that they could bite those dicks off, bite those oh that feels so good baby down your throat daddie's little cocksucker oh you're a real good cocksucker suck on that big piece of meat, I wish they could tear at that little bit of flesh stuck between those homophoby hairy thighs, pull it away with their teeth and show the big man how a queen deals with a man that's gotten a little too big.

In Greece, the country roads are lined with homemade shrines for those killed on the curves and intersections. Those people have a memory of themselves left in tin boxes filled with oil and bread and old wedding photos and drawings of The Virgin. I think that we should start erecting shrines on the streets of this city for those that will never be remembered, for the children that work these roads and are killed by an accident that may not be an accident. We should start planting black rods, tall black steel rods in the paving of these streets until they become impassable from all the memories, until New York looks like a pin cushion with all the thorns of these children sticking out of it. In my country, we can't remember too distinctly by leaving personal mementoes that affix a face to death. All we can leave are monuments even though we yearn for the morbid specificity that the Greeks embrace when they lay a battered hat or a lock of hair or a wedding veil or a child's toy in tin boxes along the road that strangers can peer into like personal diaries and know that one individual with certain tastes and experiences was cared for and not forgotten and was mourned after an unexpected death took them. In America we make monuments and I want a monument not made of polished marble, not here. I want a monument in this city that slams a steel rod in its exposed back for every one of us that falls and will never have a name. I want to remember this hurt years from now while I lean against the cold wall of an abandoned building near the river and know that something horrible and beautiful happened before my eyes. Even if I can't remember their names and faces by seeing a photo or a leather jacket or an earring in a little tin box on stilts, I want to remember this pain.

In the distance some cops have pushed two drag queens and a young Puerto Rican stud up against a wall and are frisking them, particularly the Latino guy. Their hands move over and over his body as it becomes clear that there is nothing to find but he is forced to take off his shirt for a closer frisk by New York's finest. Their hands keep moving over that hairless brown torso and I imagine that they linger particularly over the fine nipples and under his arms as they bark insults into his ear, asking him about his two girlfriends and how would he like to watch the girlies get two big nightsticks up their asses. Two ruddy white thick men going over three brown bodies in a broken down street. They must have forgotten their badges at home, these cops. They must have forgotten their name tags at home, these cops. They must always leave a little something at home on the dresser when they go out to do what they know is wrong but they're able to do it because of that polished piece of metal, that trophy which is left where it won't be soiled when they go out nightly to dishonor the job they're paid to do. Their wives or mothers or sisters or any other available female slave stays at home to polish the little shield badge and to be oh so proud of their big public defender while that same hairy assed man is slapping around a drag queen who hasn't eaten in two days so gets two cop cocks for dinner. I turn down the side street before the deal is worked out in the back of the cop car that will involve mouths and asses and two white dicks getting worked over for free followed by an arrest that was promised to be averted by a little sucking and fucking.

Passing white caverns of trucks, rows of white metal arranged to create gorges, caverns, hiding places for those who must remain hidden in urban shadow. Trucks sticky with just dried blood and full of the smell of the slaughtered, they pay for their sins by housing a different cargo by night. And now some of the queens manage to nap away from the chill and how quiet and young they look rolled up into little balls, two to a cab. Like all people, the queens get younger while asleep and being only fifteen or sixteen anyway they look like abandoned babies, resting, leaning one against the other for some warmth and comfort. They either do not notice or are too tired to comment upon the men that slide between the narrow valley walls of metal as I do now, glimpsing an arm in leather pulling at a denim ass before rolling under a truck and gone. Feet pad steadily through the maze and I follow their sounds and one man's body draws me particularly with its round hard ass stretching to the limit a tattered pair of Levis.

He is past 30, possibly past 40, with a face that is impossible to judge. The beard is a bit too long and the jacket a bit too new for the typical player I find here and it may be that this man is one of the many that has come here not for sex but for hate, to inflict his hate on the innocent because he cannot accept his life. I step slowly toward him with the thought that each morning I read of men like myself that left their homes one night and without looking for it found the flesh slipping off their faces and metal pushed through their skin and became another piece of meat for the workers to dismantle the next day or maybe they were simply absent, unfound the next day and the following and they remained missing but barely missed.

The times I've run with blind fear down these dark
Village streets escaping men who hate, hate with
such vehemence that they are beyond bigotry. Such
men, and almost always men, attain what was called
evil hundreds of years ago. This evil travels in packs
because it is cowardly and these packs roam like a
modern Inquisition, rooting out difference and
stretching it until the sinews of soft flesh begin to
tear and scream and repent. And it's the same team,
ever young, which moved through Germany and
Ireland and Greece and Africa and moves yet now in
Louisiana and Iowa and Brooklyn. The simple act of
sliding the long knife in my pocket, at the ready,
turns the tables. Because as my flesh is scraped from
the bone so will theirs be, as my face scars and flaps
open, so will theirs and as I cry and scream when help
is just too far away, so will they. So I'll walk towards
this man's dark, hairy body with a little less fear
tonight, and less fear tomorrow.

Oh, the hard mounds of his ass and he barely
moves, moves not at all now as I feel over those
cheeks. Your face is averted as it should be and you
don't look but now I wish you to, wish you to let your
heavy lidded eyes to drop down to mine so that I can
see hate or lust or affection or camaraderie or hate.
But your face is averted as it should be and only your
rock hard body is here to slam against now, an unreal
marble and that hard ass of yours will open and
swallow me if it wants to. Each part of this denim
body has a separate existence and the ass and tits

can converse with one another or my hands as my lips suck but do not speak to your beard. I want this body to fall apart, I do not want your eyes now but dismembered parts of a body that belongs to no one man but is archetypical in the way the cheek meets the beard line and the hair curls upward on the incline of the chest. My lips are taking your body apart one area at a time until you are barely human and I'm here again alone.

This big hairy man is pushed back against a truck now by my small body and I'm sucking his tits until I'm sure they're about to bleed. He may still be a killer but now he's controlled for the moment and as my mouth works his chest he wonders how far to let this go, if my lips should get him off and then what, at this hour, then what when it's time to go home already and another night done too soon. But his groin and his mind are not communicating and the hairy white thighs are grinding on me while I leave teeth marks all over his chest. "Time to go," as I shove him back harder against the truck, slapping his chest. "Time to go," I whisper again to him as I grab his face and pull it towards mine and I know that when I push my tongue into his mouth he'll come whether he wants to or not. This is the best way to start the evening. I've made the right choice tonight as he starts to shake and my body is calm and my cock not even out of my pants as he trembles and cream drips down his leg. He makes no move to pull his pants up from the pool of tepid water they dip in or to say a small inanity or to move in any way acknowledging this is over and as I move away from his black and white and red chest, I look back to see him standing still flung against the truck, leaning over at the abdomen as if someone had punched him hard in the gut.

This man was a cocktail to set the tone for the remainder of the evening. He relaxed me by letting go control of his body and handing himself over to a stranger. He trusted the strong direction my hands led him in. I can wipe his sperm from my hands without remembering anything about him but his red chest. Ready now. The maze of trucks falls away as I walk down the middle of the cobblestone street to the club that is only now beginning to fill with men. The Hook, so named for the shape of its basement, is one of the few clubs that has come forward to replace The Mineshaft and The Anvil. At best, it's a sanitized version of its predecessors, necessarily considering the sexual and political implications of AIDS. What remains most important to the atmosphere of the place, however, is not the type of sex that goes on but the mental state of disorientation and calm that it induces. By 2:00 the men begin to arrive but not until well after 4:00 when the bars close is it packed enough so that the proper abandon is possible.

It is marked on the street only by a harsh white yard light that announces only whether the club is open, but not who it is open to. The facade is of diagonal slabs of wood, fitted together loosely so that the smell of sweat leaks out to join other sweat on the street. There is never any sign of activity outside these places because the men come singly and discretely, slipping or striding in quickly, the decision of whether to come or not having been made long ago. I hate the few men who do come in pairs or little groups to add support to their big adventure and then stand about inside, smug, thinking they're not like me, that they don't spend the evening alone, isolated from conversation. But I know. I know that those men think only of losing the group, sneaking away so that anonymous hands can grab their tits and balls until it doesn't matter who it is, who those hands belong to, just so they go on without speaking.

This man that works the door, I wonder about him and the others that actually make their living here. Do their jobs of taking money and prying apart the dangerously amorous become as mundane as mine? Routine can transform any act into boredom but this man pulls a pair of leather chaps over his legs before he goes to work and slips metal rings through his nipples and can that really be the same as my feet trodding slowly over the pavement each day with the same layer of black wool clothes worn day after day? I would be too afraid to demystify these places by working in them or perhaps it's that I would be completely swallowed by this life. Tom, the man that takes the money, has the blankest eyes I've ever seen. They are brownish black with thick brows overhanging them but they always seem completely colorless as if I could look through them to the back of his skull. It's not that he's stupid but that he no longer thinks. I don't know the particulars of his life but he seems to have found happiness in the way that a lobotomized patient finds happiness, in emptying the brain into a bowl and then looking intently at things one can no longer see. I've had sex with Tom several times here. Invariably I find him sitting down, off duty, on a low bench and as I walk towards him he looks up with those blank, pleading eyes which draw my hands downwards to his smooth skin. His head sinks down again as I stroke his back like an obedient dog and then reach under to draw him up by his nipples, against the wall. Those eyes bring out a gentleness in me.

I'm in despair when I push aside the long strips of industrial plastic that cover the door. Empty, still empty. It's the waiting part of looking for sex that I can't take. Hours of waiting in these slimy dives before a few moments of getting off. God, if I counted the wasted hours spent leaning against a wall in one of these places fighting off boredom and depression watching the same porno movies I've seen a thousand times. Always the same porno of two hairless men in a locker room sniffing at each other's ass. But I won't judge yet as the real action is downstairs and there may be a few lurking below. The Hook really wins the award for the darkest of these places with even the bar area only illuminated by only a few blue spots and the glow of the jukebox which plays a song I've never heard before, "We'll be together again. I've been waiting for a long time. We'll be together again." I'm skipping the bar area and moving directly downstairs. I have no patience tonight.

The basement of The Hook is a masterpiece. It really looks like somebody's basement in a house in the Midwest. John Wayne Gacy's basement probably looked like this. I surmise all mass murderers have completely J.C. Penney houses with shag carpets and everything in coordinated earth tones. They sit around their mass murder, mail-order houses in velour sweat suits or terry cloth robes and watch the Family Feud or Wheel Of Fortune while they try not to think about their basements. They try oh so desperately to keep their minds on Entertainment Tonight while the locked door of the basement rattles on its hinges. That fucking basement is alive. Some stupid Midwestern man turned mass murderer has made his fucking basement come alive in the middle of Iowa. At first all he did was paint it black and it seemed out of place and creepy but after all it's only paint. But then every piece of furniture was cleared out and thrown away, every decoration removed and every wall torn down until one black room remained. There are no fluorescent lights in the basements of killers, you can bet on that. There are spotlights like they use in high school theater productions that are really only blue bulbs focused by black cardboard tubes held in place by duct tape. Those lights don't point down because there's nothing to illuminate, no furniture, no books to read. Those lights are always steeply angled to shine in eyes, to glare against the black gloss of the walls. Mass murderers are universally drawn towards their basements and so are the little boys that are drawn downwards by the sexual charge felt there. And once one of the bodies of those little boys falls apart down there, that fucking basement changes and it's not a basement in the middle of Iowa any more, it's a chapel with black marble walls and sacred silver instruments and drones from an organ in the mosaic vaulted chambers above. Someone who understands mass murderers designed the basement of The Hook.

The lights blaze in my eyes but do not light the room. I can see that there are a fair number of men down here. I'm not ready yet. Just to the side of the stairway is an alcove where sex rarely happens but is dark enough to take care of private matters. I drop the heavy leather of my jacket to the floor and unbutton my shirt so that it falls off me but is suspended by being tucked into my jeans. With my jacket on again the skin of my chest is so white that I stroke it, feel its warm smoothness. In my pocket I find two of the black market Quaaludes which are increasingly hard to come by these days. What an incredible drug Quaaludes, the sloppiness of a severe drunk without the nausea and depression. I've developed a talent for taking pills without water and they slip down my throat easily, hitting my empty stomach. Without food in my stomach I will feel the drug very quickly and I rest here for a moment waiting for my body to begin feeling stretched and rubbery and numb. I remember falling down the stairs of the old Ice Palace high on a Quaalude drunk and laughing all the way down. That was a long time ago.

The white curve of an ass draws me across the room to another small alcove with a beat-up vinyl couch. There's not a hair on this man's body, he's shaved off every hair and the shock of the uncovered skin is painful, severe. He scuttles like a little crab towards the couch and then away again, clutching at his ass and muttering when anyone seems to be approaching. Back again to the couch he goes, peering over large glasses suitable for an accountant, making sure I'm really heading his way. Now I hear him as he sticks his ass up to the air, kneeling on the couch, "I'm an asshole. Asshole." Squeaky, quavery voice. But the bareness of his body is irresistible to my hands and they move down to his tits and pull him up roughly, evoking the start of a scream which is suppressed, his eyes rolling as he relinquishes his chest and ass and mouth to me. "Thank you, sir. I'm an asshole." I shove him back over and kick his legs apart, far apart and then farther as his hole twitches, losing that last bit of control. His ass does not redden as I slap it hard, waiting, slapping again at irregular intervals so that he doesn't know when the next blow will land. It will not redden even though my hand aches and itches from use. It stays cold and firm and white, twitching for more. Each blow, harder than the last is met with, "Thank you, sir. I'm an asshole." This man, this accountant has transformed himself into a waiting ass, dropping the other parts of his body until nothing but sensation from that hairless ass tells him he's alive. He wins when he doesn't want to win because his control of the situation is total, whatever I do will please him, whatever I do will evoke the same response. He owns the master, conquers the torturer. I leave him, legs spread, muttering.

My cock's half hard from the cold leather rubbing my nipples as I glide across the floor. Those lights. I can't see the men and I go past them again and again watching their rubbing hands, their white and brown bodies. Stumble and on again back to the curve of the room, to the sharp point of the hook where the room narrows, shoving all bodies toward the center. Someone has me, literally has me. My right arm is pulled sharply up behind me and my left is pinned against my side. A body which is compact and bold holds me here grinding its crotch against my ass. And suddenly releases me, leaving my arms hanging in their restrained positions without pressure.

There is a face along with that body and the body is quite as I thought it would be with large, firm tits lightly covered with hair which gives way to a bare stomach rounded with muscle and some fat. He is flexing his muscles for me but it isn't ridiculous, not a show but an invitation. His name is Ty, the name of some boy in my childhood, a strange name derived from Tyler or Tyrone or another name that no one really uses. "Show it to me, man," he flexes out the words along with his movements and he wants me to join him, to start moving my body, which is beginning to feel very loose, in a way so that blood will pump up the muscles, curve the skin, distend the stomach. Rather I feel along the incredible arch of his biceps and rub the breasts till the nipples harden. He's an old man with a young man's body. Only a young man's body in this light and I forget what the color of the skin would turn to under the lights of an office or a market. I forget what an old man is and change it into a mark of power. "Show it to me, man." I rub our chests together as he sticks a popper up my nose.

That odor. The horror stories of chemicals inducing labor in livestock, the mutating DNA, my tongue lapping an arm. That odor is my name and my sex in a brown medical bottle labeled abandon and we do abandon as we are abandoned and slip into little brown bottles of unlabeled pungent aroma. No longer will I avoid this risk. I cannot so don't ask, don't rip away a dance learned to music from far off and translated into this language of moving hips and grinding faces and a focus narrowing to one square inch of man's skin. Take me now and don't speak not now what to say in this spinning black room below ground we're submerged into one another and you are a man without a face and without a name and you have one arm, you have one arm and that arm is full within my view. You are a man with an arm which can control me as it does as it turns me and pulls me and my long cloak thrown to the side and flesh begins to wetten as you hold me back against the wall of you. You are a man who tells me to flex, tells me to tighten and holds me as others even more faceless, even more nameless, others not even human lick and chew at the exposed me as you hold and wetten me while they work without talk. You are a man who whispers of my beauty as you hold my limp body as a trophy on display, a safari prize your large arms brought down suddenly and you take possession of me, grind me and swallow me with little effort as others of the pack devour the front of my body which has left me now. That odor drives me past where I know and that odor is repeated beyond safe measure as your hands feel up inside me and shake this limp rag doll with muscles rippling and subsiding as they are pushed along by anonymous tongues. You are a man who has stopped time as the sun rises but not here in this utter blackness as the hours swirl past me along with a parade of bodies that sample of me and leave and return again from the depths of this black room which is so huge that I will never see the far limits of it where perhaps rays of light struggle through cracks and make my skin soft and glistening with wetness from tongues and backs and areas beyond. You are a man who leaves me finally spent and whispers bravely in my ear, "Don't be afraid to compete, man, don't you ever be afraid to compete."

WEDNESDAY

I woke up this morning to find my crotch full of small animals. Crabs, which used to disgust me, now are simply a bore. The routine of sitting around with foul A-200 lotion smeared all over your body while the bed clothes soak in a bleach wash is one of the less glamorous components of a heavy sex life. Do they scream in their own private crab language as the poison washes over their small bodies or do they tighten and tighten their scaly armor trying to deflect the scalding fluid until the battle exhausts them or do they simply fade from consciousness with a calm unknown to human suffering? This is a fitting way to start a day that will be capped by going to work early this evening where human parasites crawl all over me and suck out what remaining talent I have.

My work is artistic, I work with artists, I work as an artist. My work is as a slave in a second-rate club where I present the mess called Performance Art, or simply Performance to those in the know.

The club, Signal, squats down on the last block before the river in Chelsea which is quickly becoming a trendy neighborhood filled with large, industrial discos and museums. Only a few years ago the Chelsea waterfront was home only to the best leather bars, empty warehouses and the poor. Now hot spots for the white trendies glower behind metal riot doors and turn their backs to the colored faces that pass by them. Violence remains an integral part of Chelsea where the bodies of gay men and lesbians pile up under the hate of men who travel in packs with baseball bats and small, sleek guns looking to kill that which they desperately seek to become. Yet the artists who inhabit this thin island cling desperately to ambiguity and neutrality in the face of suffering and for this reason I detest them and their empty gestures.

Having deloused myself and pulled on a black suit with a T-shirt, I leave at about 8:00 hoping to avoid the owner of the place while I deal with the fuck-up act I've booked tonight. I met these two brothers who I had seen around a lot in a sex club a few months back and we got to talking about Signal. Turns out they're not Puerto Rican as I'd assumed but Italian. Only one of them is really attractive but both have solid bodies with smooth, smooth skin and a slight oily sheen that draws the hand towards it. As I felt up the cuter of the two, they told me they were performers with an act called Dietro which sounds ridiculous but shocking. What better qualifications than being gay brothers into heavy sex could an act have, so tonight marks their big time premiere in the world of Downtown art. Gay art is the flavor of the month here in Chelsea, here in Manhattan where there's a law against things existing for more than a minute. But for the moment, there's nothing the straighties like better than a little fag titillation, a little dance from the plague set. So we totter on stage or splatter some paint on canvas and tell them the nasty, nasty tale of our lives.

Franky is eating this evening and I mentally note this in the Franky file because I've never seen him eating before. His wide legs are planted sturdily on the floor as he leans back on his stool and balances his Styrofoam plate on his lap. I fumble getting my mail from the mailbox so that I can see what his meal is. It's a revolting mixture from what I can see, some sort of milky pickled fish which he scoops onto crackers and pops into his mouth. Bits of the crackers and fish are stuck in his thick moustache and I stare at its bristles as they move over the shifting teeth. My father would eat things like that, things pickled and canned and smelly. Sardines were his personal favorite and I was allowed to use the metal key on the can, turning it slowly till the fastener was curled round it and the lid would slip off to reveal the fish, asleep in a row. Eating has made Franky more distant than ever, I could stare at him like this for hours without any acknowledgment so I walk past brusquely, not caring if he speaks.

It's a half hour's walk to the club past warehouses and townhouses and a route I know so well I ignore it. True to form, the owner has arrived early to meddle and make trouble. Jesus, I hate the sight of him more every time I see him. A TV with long black hair and sallow skin, Ronny was great to me when I first met him. He gave me lots of room to book what I wanted, trusted my work and kept out of my way— just what an owner should do. Lately, though, since his big-dicked, 18 year old, moron lover left him this queen has turned vicious in a way that only the truly insecure can by trying to self-destruct everything around him and then spread the blame onto the employees. Now, he has decided to be little Miss Artistic with lots of studded leather jackets and big frizzy hair which seems to have a separate life and perverse agenda of its own.

The real icing on the cake though has been a series of self-generated publicity articles describing Ronny's commitment to art. He assumes that those of us who work for a living are too dumb to read and will never see these saccharine profiles written by his old tricks or distant relatives. My personal favorite was the one I ran across in *Texas Art Journal*, of all places, which gives us a tour of Ronny's typical day in the hard hitting art world. We find Ronny waking at the crack of dawn, gulping down a cup of coffee and whisking out the door in an Azzedine Alaia number to help repair the club and build sets. Meanwhile, this queen has never stumbled out of his waterbed before noon and shops at Strawberry from what I can see. Oh, the profile goes on and on, practically a novel, to the non-stop networking and late night adventures of the young and gifted. The writer must have forgotten the section telling about

Ronny's coke problem and how glamorous it is to watch him thread a cocktail straw up into his nasal cavity since his hooter's too burned out to snort anymore. Yeah, Ronny always forgets to mention those bloody cocktail straws.

Ronny informs me as my welcome this evening that I have a responsibility to Signal as a great bastion of (his words) "cutting edge performance by emerging artists" and that we must not be afraid of the extreme but have to expand our audience at the same time. In other words, the little hypocrite wants some action the Yuppies can get a thrill off of but won't freak them out. I remind him of the guy that blew a tomato juice enema out of his ass a few weeks back on stage hitting Ronny square in the face and inducing Ms. Cutting Edge to scream, "Get that fucking freak and his AIDS riddled ass out of here or I'll make you both sorry." I guess he can only deal with emerging artists, not exploding artists.

As he clickety-clicks off to his office with the heels of his pumps asserting themselves by smashing down on the floor boards with every insecure step, I wonder what it is that draws people like him to New York. Ronny, the product of a fabulously wealthy Midwestern family, is obsessed with pretending he is a starving artist and can't go ahead with the operation to chop his dick off until he saves up a lot more money, even though he regularly stocks up on the latest electronic doo-dads for his clunky little apartment. I imagine him hiding all the Sanyo and Toshiba and Sony and Yamaha products under his bed and putting up Philip Glass posters when company is expected. There seems to be a new trend in Manhattan of the affected poor, the ones with big fat bank accounts that they keep hidden while they run sleazy businesses and rip off their employees. These faux poor have decided to infiltrate the arts community in New York and transform it from something ugly but real into a shiny little package ready to be shipped to the Brooklyn Academy of Music for purchase by the next carnivorous corporate entity waiting in line for respectability via support of the arts.

The Dietro brothers have arrived before me and Ronny seems to be leaving them alone while they set up but I can see him glancing out of his door now and then to get a view of their round asses as they stoop over strewing the stage with dead flowers. They do have magnificent bodies which they promise are going to be on full view during the act. Little do the poor things realize that their dressing room doubles as Ronny's office and he'll be demanding a preview. They move really slowly around the stage handling the grey flowers with great seriousness and placing them precisely in spots that make a pattern only they understand the significance of. Occasionally they'll move to the side and lightly hold hands while they kiss and discuss something in Italian. I can't hear all of the words but the better looking of the two keeps shaking his head and looking down as if he's being unjustly scolded. His huge brown eyes peer over to me, saying that I understand, that I know his misery. What would it be like to hold that sculpted body of his and let him cry for hours on end? Just let him weep like the tortured kid he is and never have sex with him but lay him over my lap with folds and folds of blanket up around him in a long Pieta.

I finally tell them that we're going to open so they should change and show them into Ronny's office where he's staring at the wall and acting aloof as if he had too much to worry about to talk to ordinary mortals. The boys take it in stride so I tell the DJ to hit the lights and music and the woman working the door tonight starts letting people in. The woman at the door is this great dyke who doesn't go for any of the "pick and choose" bullshit that happens at a lot of New York clubs. She just lines them up and packs them in as efficiently as possible, talking constantly as she does it and offering good advice when asked. Tonight she's got on a basic white shirt that shows off the strong outline of her torso and a pair of well-worn black jeans. There were a lot of people like her in New York when I first came here, not uptight or competitive or showy, but they seem to be a vanishing breed and are being replaced by idiots that are just out to make some money but who weren't good enough to be a lawyer or a doctor or something. This particular woman shares an Irish heritage with me and it's always been a bond between us even though I could give a shit which hamlet my ancestors came from. Sometimes I think I'm her and I'm playing softball in Brooklyn or rowing down the East River thinking, yes, I could be her, I could be strong and friendly instead of withdrawn and weak. Even though it's only a long deleted blood pool, I'm glad something ties me to a person like her.

The crowd seem marginally hipper than usual tonight with the sense that everyone knows everyone else and they're all worth knowing. Ever since Warhol finally tossed his wig and croaked, his old pack has been showing up in force making sure that, yes, they did know Andy very well, very, very well and Andy was faaaabulous to work with as he did, very often and very well, with them. God, there must be ten of those tired old Warhol warhorses here tonight and we're not talking Edie Sedgewick but the marginally affiliated, the Andy wannabes who rolled into his apartment one night with a big wig on and decided they were a star. I'm going to start a rest home for these people, ship them off to the Andy Memorial Home in Scarsdale where they'll have false eyelashes applied every morning before their oatmeal and granola snacks and then there'll be a good two, three hours of name dropping, with Andy being the most frequently dropped naturally, before lunch.

There's a woman in the crowd tonight that I keep staring at because she seems so out of place. What's strange isn't that she seems to know a lot of people and they keep flocking around her like an entourage, but that they are all such different types ranging from a fashion designer covered in disheveled black and safety pins to an incredible drag queen sheathed in sequined bondage gear to several intellectual literary types. She's not a celebrity, at least one that

I recognize, but she looks rather like one of those movie stars from the forties with an elegant but simple little dress revealing thin, thin legs and an ivory colored face with an elaborately patterned scarf covering her hair. My best friends have always been women and hopefully not just for the stereotypical fag reasons but also because they can teach me things without being scathing and have things to teach me, both personal and political, which I desperately wish to know. Many of these relationships have ended badly though, with me coming off as grasping or bored or both.

"You know a lot of people here," I start in, not knowing what the point of the conversation will be. But it turns out that it's very comforting talking to someone so self-assured who can command a roomful of people with small mannerisms. She's very fragile and it fascinates me that in this city she would have chosen to actually cultivate this breakable quality while frequenting clubs located on streets covered with pigeon shit and sodden garbage. It seems that she's some sort of actress and has worked in New York for a long time, although she looks really young. She's going on and on with a very complicated and funny story about her mother and while she's describing how her mother once showed up at a party in a dress made of astro turf, she pushes the scarf back off her head. Her hair is very blond, almost white and I don't think I've ever seen anyone who is so uniformly pale with every surface of her body seeming like it could be easily dirtied by her surroundings. I've had very few close friends in my life

51

but I think that this woman could be one and lately I've become much more excited at the prospect of a loyal friend than by anything else. It's past 9:00, when the performance is scheduled to begin and I excuse myself after asking her to call me so we can talk further.

I knock on the door of Ronny's office but no one answers. Squinting through the blinds on the door I can make out Ronny's bulbous hair bobbing up and down on the lap of one of the boys as he blows him and the other brother looks like he is snorting some of Ronny's coke on the desk, all of them looking calm and bored. After listening to Ronny's boring platitudes about the experimental art world they were probably happy to shut him up even if it meant plugging his throat. I can just imagine the smacking, sucking sound coming out of Ronny's throat and the candy red lipstick smeared all over that beautiful cock. What a waste. The DJ has started the slow smashing tape the brothers brought and the cute one pulls his fat dick out of Ronny's mouth and they open the door. "Wait till the lights dim before you go up on stage," I say while I lead them through the crowd and behind a tattered curtain.

Just as they're about to begin up the stairs onstage, Ronny pushes past them brusquely and takes to the microphone. Not again. He pulls himself up before the audience, quite a feat considering he's only 5' 3" and tugs firmly down on his long black wig, "I want to take just a moment of your time before we introduce our act this evening to say a few words about the state of the arts as I see them." There are a few loud groans from the audience. I can't believe he insists on doing this, assuming that anyone could possibly care about what this little pretender, this little upstart would have to say about the arts or dicksucking or any other subject. "We have a responsibility to ourselves to support artists who are making bold new strokes on the canvas of culture, to move with them, to help them hold their painter's brush. Our support of them must be unequivocal at every juncture. Signal presents for you the best of the contemporary experimental arts in a setting which is invigorating but responsive to the needs of the artistic community. I ask you all to continue your support of these fine performers because whether you happen to like one act or another is beside the point, the fact is that we are creating a community which encompasses all points of view. Remember, when you support Signal you support your community." I love the resounding boos Ronny's instructive lecture receives as he clicks back down the stairs with his head thrown back and rudely shoves past me back to his office for another line of coke.

Video monitors on stage blink on showing a tape the two have made of nature shots, lots of brownish gray trees and flowers with blooms in putrid colors zooming in and out of focus. When the lights come up I can see that they've covered their bodies in a fine white powder and it makes the curves of their biceps obscenely beautiful as they stagger toward the microphone, pulling at the dirty pouches that cover their dicks and balls. The cute one looks like he's about to start some speech but he motions to the DJ to raise the volume of the screeching tape. You can hear only portions of what he's screaming into the mike while his brother whispers continually into his ear from behind, "Five bloody cats are clawing at me...ripping at my balls...punch fuck me hard...Get these fucking furry monsters off my face...it's not my fault...I dug up all those flowers, not in bloom, dormant...they were weeds, not catnip, not roses...how to know...call them off...Call off your vicious attack cats...good pussy, good pussy, good little puss...They didn't bloom...never did but leaked blood and cum at midnight after you'd gone to bed...left me with the weeds and all those cats rub, rub, rubbing those weeds...matted fur matted from the weedy blood cum...Can you expect me to look at that while you sleep and snore...Hoe up those rose weeds...rip 'em up, rip 'em up out your stomach...I'll take those pukin' weeds out your stomach with a hoe and those cats can do what they will mad as hell...Slam me solid up to the minute I stop thinking these thoughts...Roman alleyways filled with starving, screaming cats...fuck me down to the level I belong with two sweaty shits rubbing over dead weeds and dead bloody cocks...Slice serve me up to the strays... feed the hungry, Lord, with my poor life...don't tear...enough of my miserable cock to go around... enough to fill all of your growling tummies with the putrid meat of my soul...Pray for us...pray for us, for all who inhabit this city of retching hate...pray for our souls to survive this which they were not meant to endure...Penance begins now...penance...to pay...pray for me." They've started kicking the flowers and whipping at one another with the long brittle stems of them. The ugly one punches his brother hard in the chest, leaving a pink smear where the flour was. "Thank you Lord for this blessing...dead decay of compost...of small withering love...die for me...die for me..." Their beautiful bodies are opening fully to accept each other's slamming fists and blood and ugly purple welts start to cover large sections of the heaving white torsos. The cute one has reached some sort of ecstatic state now and does not defend himself but continues his happy wail into the mike as his brother slaps him around the face and crotch. "Fuck this loving Jesus with sharp hands...repent...repent...I do repent the sin of the loving Jesus with sweet blood flowing out from... take the bloody holy cock and Lord it down my unwelcome throat." His face looks so happy now with the blood rippling down it as he weeps and partially collapses in front of his brother. The music, which has been extraordinarily loud to the point of pain, begins to fade. He's so happy, grateful for what his ugly brother does to him and in the moments when the lights are still on but very low I see him continuing to move his lips very quickly but I don't hear what he's saying anymore.

Some night I'm taking that little boy, bloody red little boy, away from his brother and to my house where it's very cool and still. Into the white tiled bath and the steam rolls up over his firm boy muscles and his pores open to the air and let go their dirt and shame. He'll close his eyes, this Italian boy as I whisper to him in his language about how we're leaving this city, returning to Rome and we'll live on a quiet piazza where the old ladies in black nod in the windows and an elderly Communist owns the neighborhood trattoria. I'll tell him all this in my bad Italian as the water gurgles higher and higher in the tub, his body floating up in the liquid. Yes, we'll find another life, away from this city, and Rome won't be as he remembers it, with crowds and soot from the screaming cars. No, Rome will be quiet again, like in the movies from the sixties where lovely blonde ladies sit on seafoam sofas wearing pale, pale grey silk. It's all right, little boy, I'll say, we're leaving here soon.

The houselights come up abruptly along with some music to cover the hissing of lots of people walking out to show their high-minded disapproval but I know they'll tell all of their advertising agency co-workers all about it tomorrow with little giggles to show how naughty and New Yorky they've been with their slumming adventures. The ones that aren't walking out as quickly have stupid grins which say, "Boy, was that stupid but I'll pretend to like it because it was cool." The pale woman passes me on her way out, bravely shaking my hand and says, "I'll call you tomorrow so we can talk." Ronny walks past and says, "You're fired."

THURSDAY

"You think you can fuck me up? You wouldn't even know where to start. You can't fuck me up because I can do it so well myself. I know how to screw myself seven ways to Sunday. I've spent my whole life self-destructing and it's a talent that grows with age. Too goddamn late to stop now. So I should stop my life now and start over? I'll go so low that you can't even see me, so low that you can't hurt me, so low that I'm untouchable. I'll go so low that you'll be amazed."

I woke up screaming again this morning. This habit scares me more than any other. There must be a terrible rage bordering on insanity inside a person to force their mouth open from a deep sleep shrieking a hate that can rip apart a peaceful room. For that person there is little hope of companionship or even momentary intimacy because for that person bitterness is the only lover available. Sex is a release for most people, but for me each orgasm builds upon the last and feeds on me until my body lies so tense in bed that it seems I'll break, that my limbs and my cock and my head will simply shatter from my torso if the pain becomes any more intense. And when I wake, half remembered phrases of hate litter the bedclothes.

Narcotics are a really marvelous gift as far as I'm concerned. Two Fiorinals will lull me back to sleep for the rest of these garish daylight hours. Every night before I go to bed, two of them are laid carefully on the dark wood of the nightstand, ready in case I wake and the pain is too crippling to allow me to get up. Two dusty white pills are always waiting for me in their faithful, inanimate way so that after about thirty minutes they start to roll through my bloodstream caressing my muscles and clenched jaw and licking at my temples. The sleep of drugs does not eliminate dreams, it simply represses them so that they are lost the instant your eyes roll open in their sockets. What a beautiful, peaceful respite two little pills can give me on mornings like these when there is little hope for employment or a career or even a way to get to sunset. Pills are my downfall, so clean, so easy and colorful. I'll never have to worry about shooting smack or coke because of the needles, couldn't bear it what with the mess and risk of infection. Pills make me feel upper class, very Park Avenue, like the downtown Brenda Frazier. Even alcohol with its social allure pales next to these white and blue and pink and red saucers.

When I wake again, it is not with screaming but with a slovenly look at the red glowing numbers of my bedside clock counting down the seconds until

8:00 p.m. The only clear things in the room are the red numbers and the blinking red light on the answering machine which has been faithfully receiving calls but keeping them quiet since the sound is turned down and the telephone ringer is off. I reach down and push the message erase button which registers with a whirring sound as it wipes away all the intruding voices. I can't bear talking today and explaining last night's disaster to consoling friends who will offer career advice. The whole idea of a career makes me sick, almost sicker than the fuzzy details of my adventures after I left Signal last night. People waste their whole lives working on careers and talking to one another's answering machines. Better to just lie here.

Something's got to break inside of me, some crisis has to pass before I can get on with my life. As I watch television this evening, it seems that the entire world is approaching this turning point as well. At certain times in history, the entire globe has sensed that there is a decision to be made which means going on or coming to an end and it may be that eventually it is time to come to an end. The violence on the screen has taken on a weariness from being acted out so many times, from the continual slashing at one another until violence becomes nothing more to me than a metaphor for my own problems. It's come to the point that if I rammed a knife through my bowels it would hurt me no more than the bleeding wounds I watch on television hurt me. Perhaps it's the pain of my community that finally snapped off the switch inside of me that says "Experience Hurt". In New

York, one can watch the news from 5:00 to 11:30 without pause. I usually start out with the "light" news at 5:00 and work my way up to the bloody, gory extravagance of the national report. With the remote control, you can switch quickly back and forth between stations to see the same image of horror again and again. And they show them shamelessly, the disasters. If there's a slow motion close-up of a decapitation or a train crash or an earthquake swallowing buildings, you can be sure that all three networks will be showing it simultaneously two or three times. Then the cut back to the blank face of Tom Brokaw or Dan Rather staring you in the eyes saying, "Don't care about this. Close down. Don't care. It isn't real."

As the evening progresses I invariably end up watching Manhattan Cable's Public Access channels and tonight the lineup pits my two favorites against one another. Hitting the flashback button on the remote control I switch between Robin Byrd on Channel J and Coca Crystal on Channel A. Robin was once the queen of cable, with her damaged blonde hair hanging in her eyes and a macrame bikini caught in her crotch she introduced weary Times Square dancers as if they were stars. For a few minutes they were stars as Manhattan watched them struggle out of their clothes, wet a forefinger in their mouths and lower it seductively to their groins. Lately I've mostly defected from Robin due to her overpopularity with stupid people and have devoted more time to the cable purism of Coca. Coca's show mixes boredom with bizarreness so that by the end of an hour you feel like you've lived with her. She just picks up her life and transplants it into a sleazy studio complete with nauseating tofu recipes, non-stop pot smoking and her mentally handicapped son zooming around the set. I can never remember the name of her son but it's something like Sam or Zachary or Jeremy and really the best thing about him isn't when he comes in the frame of the camera but when he starts talking in his own private language in the corners of the set. Only Coca understands what his wailing sounds mean and I have a feeling it's more from an emotional link between them than actual recognition of the words. I often think about Coca and Sam/Zachary/Jeremy at home and Coca might be making a simple tempeh-burger dinner with her son wailing with happiness and I wonder what will become of him when Coca finally croaks. There's always that pretentious old avant garde queen that takes emotionally disturbed children and has them write down 10,000 pages of their most relevant thoughts on Renaissance Art, makes it into a slow motion play and then calls himself a genius. But of course he doesn't have sex with them and it's just a coincidence that they're all boys, like there isn't one handicapped girl on earth. Maybe Sam/Zachary/Jeremy could turn out to be a real gold mine for Coca.

Tonight Coca has a special guest to share her continuous supply of fat joints with. This guy apparently is the new shining light of the gay theatre and from the looks of things his mother was a ball of cheese and his father a pig. I mean this guy is ugly, not that I mind people being ugly but this guy is really pushing it and is stupid to boot. He's puffing on Coca's joint so that these balls of smoke are rolling up without him possibly having the chance to inhale and his skin looks like cheddar cheese when it sits out in the summer with this sweaty condensation on it. Now he's off on how gay theatre should be uplifting and happy instead of wallowing in the sorrow of the AIDS crisis and the more he describes his happy new musical about Kaposi's Sarcoma the more desperate he looks until I'm sure he's about to have a break-down of joy. This asshole is driving me to do some-thing I hate to do which is to dial the call-in number that all of these shows have. I guess no one is watch-ing tonight because I get through and before Coca can even take another toke I start in, "Listen, Coca, I used to think you were really cool and I don't mind your stupid health food recipes and I don't mind your retarded kid but this playwright asshole is the end. Hey, asswipe, since you're so happy about AIDS maybe you could get off your fat butt to go demonstrate or something instead of blowing your own horn about your latest gay version of 'Laverne and Shirley'. Because you know what, I'm fucking depressed about this disease and I'm depressed about the gay community and I'm depressed that there are people out there that want to kill us. So you can take your dancing, singing lesions and shove them up the asses of all those other cabaret queens who want to pretend that this isn't the most horrible thing that ever happened because if I want to be mad and anti-social and fight with people and say things are completely screwed up in this city I will and I'll say it all over your ugly, cheesy face."

Coca's completely horrified by this outburst and her ratty little face juts through the cloud of pot smoke towards the screen. The playwright's looking very peeved and starts to get up when Coca cuts in, "You know, mister, you think you're the only person that's ever had a problem. You think your group is the only group that's ever had a hard time. Maybe you should think about some other people sometimes like Jewish people or black people or women. Cause I can tell you, buddy, that we all have problems and it's not a big deal. Why don't you just fucking relax and let my guests have their points of view instead of coming out with these Fascist tactics."

She's obviously very satisfied with her response and I'm backing away from the screen with the phone in my hand, "Well, thanks for that advice Coca. And I'll take it to heart because you're one person who obviously has had her share of problems. What with taking so much shit that your kid came out brain damaged and having this flea bitten cable show and waxing philosophical about the time you gave Abbie Hoffman a blow job, it seems like just about everything in your life is fucked. But there is one good thing about you and your show, Coca, and that's that I can just turn you off." Coca's face or the ghost of it stays for a moment on the TV, the glowing picture tube still beaming out the hatred her eyes directed at me.

I'm out of this apartment for tonight. I'm out of

here. It's barely past 10:00 but I can't take it in here anymore. I can't take watching this little box and that being my only connection to things. No shower, no nothing but out into the streets past Franky and I don't care whether he ever says hello to me or respects me because he's just a fucking doorman nobody. Washington Square is so bright tonight I can hardly look at it without my head vibrating. What are those lights for? The dealers seem to appreciate them when they're counting cash. The homeless must find them convenient for late night reading. What disaster has struck this city I used to love so much? The deformed and maimed drape the streets with their misery, black plastic garbage bags have been ripped or chewed open and their trash strewn in wide arcs to cover the pavement. Here comes a young black man with one arm whittled to a stub and an older white woman picking along on homemade crutches. What has happened to my city? One night while I slept there was a great calamity below me, a huge airliner lost its engines as it circled lazily above Manhattan waiting to descend upon congested Kennedy. My radio must have flickered dimly with its distress calls which I ignored, resting, "We are coming down, we are coming down. All attempts to maneuver the aircraft have failed and we must attempt to land. We are coming down. I repeat we are coming down." Spotting the broadest runway, the plane slips slowly down towards Fifth Avenue in complete silence even as New Yorkers stand with their arms folded defying the huge bullet to strike at their impenetrable city. The passengers are bent forward preparing themselves and parents are holding babies in their laps and whispering their love. It strikes with a quiet roar. Catching a wing on the RCA Building, it begins to cartwheel downtown with the first great explosion upon grinding past the Empire State and then no more but tall balls of fire and debris rolling down the Avenue to overtake the Village and ignite its few pitiful trees and burn its cowering brownstones. All this while I lay stretched on my hard bed, oblivious to the fire that burns stories below. And now as I walk from the retreat of my home, the wreckage of that disaster surrounds my usual path. The survivors, with their slow trudging, seem hardly to have noticed that their lives and limbs have been wrenched from their bodies leaving them nothing but to walk the rubble searching for some food.

It's too early for The Hook or even much activity on the Piers so that leaves only the bookstore which in its ultimate tawdriness is actually the perfect choice for tonight. If you want to hit bottom real fast go check out your local backroom bookstore and do some browsing in the peep show booths. This particular store is all tarted up to look like a country cottage with white siding and little green gables but from about a block away you'll start getting a whiff of this place. There is an aroma which is particular to gay sex establishments and older gay bars which is unmistakable and permeates your clothes and face and hair and hands and shoes as soon as you walk through the door. The odor is made from equal parts of poppers spilled down shirt fronts, shit, sweat, cum, saliva and cologne mixed with repetition and age. I like to think of this gay smell as a fine wine with different vintages and values. The bookstore smell is a very fine vintage in that it changes and reveals levels of personality as one endures it, starting acrid but ingratiating itself eventually until it's almost comforting like the way grandmothers smell when they get too old and the powder starts to cake up on them.

I have never met a wider selection of people than at the bookstore. If you wait among these black booths long enough you'll meet every man in New York City. These men are among the most beautiful and the most hideous, the most mundane and the most psychotic. Something uniform takes over each of them, however, as they enter the room at the back of the store passing through the turnstile that clicks disapprovingly at their passage. Their movements are similar to the slow glide one sees in cruising bars but which becomes more pronounced here and is broken occasionally by a small shudder or a jerk of the head and then on they continue to make the route once more. The tall black video booths are arranged in a circle so that one moves always in the same direction, a school of fish riding the current of men gliding along to see what the offerings are this evening. The faces gaze back out at you from the flickering blue of screens which look to be far in the distance behind the silhouette of the man slouched against the wall fingering himself. Each booth is a perspective drawing with a male figure in the foreground narrowing back to the infinity point of a screen projecting only static.

There are twenty booths in this circle and tonight I will look in each of them again and again. Not that the occupants will change often, if at all, but I reexamine each man and as the desperation of the search intensifies, these men will change. Guys that I immediately dismiss on first inspection will look better after a few hours of no luck. Tonight is especially bad here. The only man I'm attracted to stays too far back in his booth for me to fully see him. He wears khaki shorts with a polo shirt and a denim jacket. His hair is black and well cut but I can't quite make out his face because a few long locks of the hair fall forward casting shadows all along his cheeks and mouth. One would think I'd simply be able to walk into the cubicle and get a close up look to decide, but there's a horrible finality when the door swings shut behind me. If my choice is not exactly right, I am immediately repulsed and the repulsion somehow freezes me there unable to say something quickly and leave without offending. I decide to wait even though I know that once one begins to stall in this place the evening becomes hellishly interminable. Better to let any hand do the work because they all feel the same once you shut your eyes. I decide to wait.

The scene used to be different here. Whereas now, the basic exchange of sex is a hand job, once anything was permitted. There was a dark basement in addition to these booths that hosted orgies that the confines of the booths prohibited. And in the booths it would have seemed a waste only to jerk off when one could fuck or suck or fist. These little black doors must have rattled on their hinges from the rampages inside. But now. Now attendants sneer at the dirty crew that takes its position each night looking for some relief. Attendants with flashlights prowl the dark corners hunting for a cock unconfined and howl with rage when they find one of their charges has been misbehaving.

As I mentioned, one finds the most unexpected people here and tonight's surprise guest is a famous German film director who is in New York making a documentary. I'm shocked to see how old and haggard he has become with his hair completely grey and his face looking too fleshy, like a rubber mask. He had made a movie I admired about AIDS several years ago but since then he's produced nothing but sentimental drivel. Some people have a limited amount of venom in them and like bees which die after having stung only once, this director was drained by putting his anger on screen. Now he's only a shell of the man who I'd met two years earlier in Central Park and had sex with. Then I was turned on by the bulk of his chest but was horrified to find that he was completely filthy underneath his clothes, smelling like shit and stale sweat. Maybe he's dying or maybe he's just gotten old. Everyone's tired of him, I wish he'd go back to Germany. I don't go to Germany to stick my face in his country's suffering so I don't see why he has to start sniffing around ours. Everything is so shiny white and flat in his country that pain is squashed along with all other emotions and unless you're Fassbinder, which he's not, it's impossible to dig people out from under the oppressive surface of matte paint and tin siding. He'll export some New York angst to Berlin to revive his floundering career.

I see many of the same faces each time I come here. One guy always has this big bag with him which crackles as he carries it along and after a while he'll put it in the corner and sit down on it, appearing to sleep. At $10 this is probably one of the cheaper places in town to sleep but it's also one of the dirtiest with cockroaches crawling the walls and slick puddles of cum and piss everywhere. Cockroaches terrify me the way nothing else can. Give me a five pound rat any day rather than one of those prehistoric monster cockroaches. God, what a disgusting animal with that shiny hard shell and those waving antennae trying to detect something edible, which in a roach's case is almost anything from insulation to coffee grounds to television wires to old pizzas. The roaches here might even live off of cum. Maybe that's why they're so big and vivacious, swinging along the walls with such verve that the owners should dress them up and name them. If I owned this place, I'd get the biggest queen cockroach and fit it with a red bustier, red heels and name it Perky Peanut. Perky Peanut would have this mini-replica of a Madonna video set and I'd teach it to do all of her routines by rewarding it with a nice bowl of warm cum every time it did the stair number from "Material Girl." Perky Peanut would draw more tourists than the Statue of Liberty. Eventually, I'd have to shut down the sex trade here, using the booths as closets for Perky's endless wardrobe. Since we have to live with the roaches, why bother with all the insecticide and swatting? Why not get rid of that stinking dog and leash up a fat, shiny roach baby sired off of old Perky Peanut?

On the merry-go-round here the hours slip past magically without me even thinking to look down at my watch. Tonight I'm ugly and many of the men do not even look up as I pass. I have to try to have a better look at that man in the shorts because the rest are completely hopeless, even uglier than me. He fondles himself as I peer into his booth and this time his hair has fallen further to the side revealing that the upper portion of his face is quite beautiful, rather like a Kennedy's with the forceful brow and the refined nose, but his mouth looks like it's been rebuilt. All around his lips there are extra layers of flesh which puff out the skin, stretching it tight, distending it so that the teeth show in a permanent snarling smile. This face has been shattered and put together again with a few pieces missing, creating a gap completed with filler leaving him with a face neatly divided into the real and the unreal. I can just imagine the smothering, puffy feel of his lips and the smell of his cigarette breath. Almost too late but I step back with a pat to his hand and continue on.

A little man follows me with a steady trudge and when I stop to lean against the wall he does the same, licking his lips and winking at me. The best thing to do is not to say anything, avoid eye contact and keep moving because he's been getting more agitated the last few stops, whispering something to me. Most men follow an etiquette which keeps them at a distance unless there is some sign of mutual attraction. Not this one though and his whispers are becoming audible, "Let me suck it. What can it hurt? You lean back and look at the movies and I'll make it feel good, feel real good. I know how to make a man feel good. You just look at the movie and enjoy a good, long suck job." A No Thanks deters him only for a few minutes. "It's not like I do this all the time but how about you just take down those pants for a few minutes and I'll make it worth your while. I'm happy and you have some cash in your pocket. How about twenty bucks to make it worth your while." His face is white, so white with a wispy moustache trembling on his lip. He draws his coat around himself asking me again. "Twenty bucks and we both have a good time. I know how to suck big dicks good, real good."

There's no place like the bookstore to hit bottom fast. You won't even see me I'll go so low. My voice is so ugly rasping out of my mouth, "No touching, no kissing. You just suck me off and it's twenty." He's pulling me off already to a booth and this is just a role I keep telling myself, this is just pretend, this is just a way to feel everything I can. "You stay right there, baby," he says feeling my pants. "Oh, that's a big one in there. That's a real big hard one you've got. Stay right there. I'm going to buy some poppers and get some quarters so you can watch the movies. I'm gonna suck that big one aren't I? You stay right there and keep that big one hard." This isn't real because if it were real I wouldn't have an erection standing here alone in this filthy booth waiting for an old man to come back and blow me for money. He's closed the door of the booth and I'm isolated, trapped. Once that flimsy door swings shut there's no going back.

The best thing to do is just to shut my eyes and wait for it to end. He's back soon and starts to whimper as he feels my dick, "Baby, those poppers are real expensive here. They're way too much here, baby, and I had to get them. I'm not bullshitting you baby but I can only afford ten. I want to give you more but I can only afford ten because I have to get home. They bleed you dry with prices here, baby, but I want to make you feel good. I got them for you. Please." Since this isn't real I just nod my head. "Oh, thank you baby 'cause I'm gonna make that dick feel real good. Just don't come too quick. Please don't come too quick." His old rickety knees must hurt squatting down there on the floor while he opens my pants and takes out my dick which is still inexplicably rock hard. I'm watching a movie of a very hairy man jerking off and I keep my thoughts on the smell of hair bushing out from under his fat white arms while the old man sticks the poppers in my nose and then goes back down to work on my dick. I don't care. The poppers make things zoom back and I can close my eyes and feel a mouth working on me. I could forget but he keeps working me towards coming and then stopping and talking, "Not yet. Please don't come yet. Please. Just tell me when you get close and I'll stop. Baby, I'm sucking that big cock, aren't I? It feels good, huh? Don't come yet." He's sucking me some more and I decide I'll just hold his head on me so he won't stop and I can come. But he starts chocking so that I have to let go and I hear a clicking noise. "I took my teeth out, honey. You don't mind, do you? 'Cause now

I'm going to suck that big dick some more. Don't come. Please don't come yet."

I'm drawing harder and harder on the poppers as I watch the movie and try not to think about the sensation on my dick. Frozen with no way out and his bony gums are chewing on my dick making me want to puke. I can't, I just can't anymore. Now I just have to come and leave quick before I get violent or something so I just push him off and masturbate fast while he's whining in my ear and touching my face, trying to feel and remember every part of me. "Please, I'm begging you. Please, don't come yet. I want that big dick. I want to be sucking that big dick for you." I must have come but the poppers have me so strung out that the bucking of my body seems separate, a part of the movie where the hairy man's body is writhing like mine and his eyes are looking out to mine and saying that he understands and he's here with me. The old man's still whimpering and putting his teeth back in his head when I get my pants up and a wet little hand pushes the ten dollar bill into my palm, "Thank you, baby, thank you. I was sucking that big dick, wasn't I baby?"

It's raining outside. A steady, cold rain which soaks my long leather coat and shoes as I stagger East. There are too many people on the streets. Why don't these people stay home with one another and sleep and watch television and lead quiet lives? My head pounds so much from those cheap poppers that I keep touching my temple to see if the veins are bulging, about to burst. I don't know what these things do to the inside of my head. I don't care so much about physical harm but what if these things are making me go insane and pretty soon there's nothing but slimy rooms where I blow anyone who asks and whimper when they leave? What if I'm sitting on a bag in that room with the roaches on me and not caring and nothing inside my head but the slow beat of the clubs? I can hit bottom so fast you'll be amazed. I can hit bottom so fast that you'll never get to me again.

A young black queen is huddled up against the wall of a jazz club. He's fat and his hair is all done up in an Al Sharpton style doo but he has this little paper cup rattling around in his hand as I come by. "Excuse me, sir," he starts in a lispy little Truman Capote voice, "do you have any change?" The ten dollar bill is still wadded up in my hand and I drop it into his cup. "God bless you, sir. Thank you."

"You're welcome," I say as I start to stumble on.

The shy little voice stops me soon enough though as he proudly declares, "Today's my birthday."

"Happy birthday."

"I wish it were a better birthday."

"I wish it were too," I say as I sink down next to him on the wet ground and start to cry.

"Don't worry, honey," he says as he holds me, "I've had worse."

FRIDAY

I've decided to put last night behind me. After all, I did make it home eventually in one piece and the experience did have a cathartic effect. In fact I feel rather rejuvenated today and actually made it out of bed before sunset, a good sign. Last night's clothes are all around the room, a stinking, soaking mess. The leather of the coat is still so wet that it stretches in my hands when I pick it up. I've laid everything over the bathtub and it sits there sullenly looking at me, dripping, taking the shape of the ledge it lays over. All the secretions, dirt, ground substances and breath that have poured over that coat have been absorbed and are invisible under its dull black surface.

Those clothes have been dragging me down like that water laden jacket. I need a real change, real clothes, real men with names. About once every two months I head uptown to Times Square to a Latin club open only on Friday and Saturdays. Zip-Zip has two types of clientele, the drag queens and transvestites who lounge around the banquettes until show time and the macho young Latinos who stand stiffly on the perimeters in their homeboy outfits. I've always believed it's better to stand out in the crowd so I show up in a suit and tie with my hair slicked straight back with grease to make it look even blacker against my white face. It usually works too. Of all the peoples of the world, Latinos have been graced with the greatest beauty both in the slope of their noses down to full mouths and the unbelievable smoothness of their compact, muscled bodies. Walking down the streets, the light brown of their arms draws me from blocks away. It's an unusual situation when one is attractive to a group which is so appealing.

Yet, I've never learned to learn their language, never learned to learn the rattling, lulling Spanish that Americans must learn eventually. We must accept that another language has gained importance in this country, that the light dry thuds of English will soon be extinct. Even so my natural laziness keeps me away from the interminable classes necessary for me to speak the first few words in a different tongue. My mind is stupid and slow and so entrenched in its patterns that I can no longer learn as I did when I was very young. We all grow more stupid with age but I worry that my memory is leaving me faster than normal. I may be one of the first to develop Alzheimer's in his twenties. Maybe in a few years babies will develop the disease, forgetting before they've learned, losing more than they take in to their set, unmovable American minds.

The blue blazer I wear tonight is by the young designer who was at Signal the other night. His clothes are slightly menacing and thrown together but combined with his beautiful fabrics they seem exactly right for this city where nothing is cheap and everything is disposable. I've never been one to admire jewelry but I always wear the ring my grandmother gave me the year before she died. People probably think it looks cheap or corny, but as is the way with such things they take on a meaning which has nothing to do with their physical presence. Only in the Midwest do they make rings like this and they sell them at the jewelers or the jewelry counter at K-Mart. Called Black Hills gold, these rings are made of three colors of impure gold twisted into the shape of grapes and their vines and their leaves. The story of the rings is that a man dying of thirst in the area found a spring around which grew a grape vine and below great deposits of gold. In gratitude for saving his life, the man declared that all of the strangely colored gold mined from the area must bear the mark of the grape.

In a blue blazer combined with a club tie and khaki pants, I look more ready for Connecticut than 38th Street and I'm sorry that Franky is off tonight and can't see me in these unusually respectable clothes. The cab shoots up Eighth Avenue unencumbered by traffic past hideous Penn Station and the Moonie hotel to the deserted stretch just below 42nd Street. This area shares none of Times Square's seedy vitality. From 6:00 on, the streets are empty with only a few hot dog joints and Blimpies open to service the welfare families that are scattered through the grim buildings. Very likely, it is a constant diet of chili dogs, salami, fries, fish sandwiches and Coke which demoralizes these people into complacency. There are no grocery stores, no bodegas, no green grocers to visit here. Suddenly, I feel I have no right here where children sit on the curbs until morning tapping their feet without much to say and nowhere to go but home. Yet I come here in a cab from an apartment that towers over these streets until they are only twinkly, scenic lights and the people are invisible. This could be any third world country but it's America and I still don't speak its language.

Zip-Zip has no sign so that one is forced to peer into every doorway until you see the mirrored stairway that leads down to the club. The mirrors have been pressed into a plaster that looks like whipped cream with little curls of foam which, for all of their soft appearance, can catch against clothes, tearing them viciously. Unlike a lot of nightspots, Zip-Zip has no crowd milling around outside no matter how crowded it is below. Only a few tough guy types lean against the wall of the hot dog stand next door, looking hostile and tossing around the word "fag" even though they'll show up inside later. This is not the neighborhood to stand around in, especially if you're wearing a skirt and a big wig. You can rate clubs in the city by how well they frisk you and the check here is the most complete I've encountered. Often, the stern face of the burly door guard looks through your pockets when he feels a suspicious outline which could be anything from a lipstick to a knife. Tonight, a guy in a white T-shirt and shorts is getting the once over and obviously has something to hide. The guard keeps trying to look in the nylon bag he's carrying and he keeps jerking back, "Get off me, bitch! That's personal property in there, get your fuckin' hands off it."

"Take it outside, sir," the guard drones, obviously tired of this scene which he's gone through too many times. "Either I look in your bag or you go outside, sir." I wouldn't be so bored, personally, if I was trying to search someone who likely had a gun or knife stashed on his person. Finally, the guy in white turns around shrieking and pushes past me back up the stairs and outside.

The security man shows no sign of recognizing me even though I come here quite often. He looks me over suspiciously, noting the jacket and tie and stares me down for a few seconds, seeing if I'll leave. When I stand my ground, meeting his long lashed eyes and giving his healthy biceps a lingering glance, he moves forward to frisk me over. I don't mind the strong, hairless hands patting at my chest and ass and move my legs accommodatingly so he can check between them. He grunts an assent and I push my cover charge through the window and walk through the turnstile.

Dirty red wallpaper meets dirty red felt meets dirty red linoleum in the interior to be broken only by strips of gilded mirrors, wrought iron curlicues and badly painted scenes from some Carnival covered in protective plastic wrap. To clean the place they must just turn on all the taps and let it flood because all the surfaces have the dull shine of dirty water washing. The crowd, however, is turned out in their weekend best that they have been sewing and appliqueing all week long. These queens spare no expense for the chance to rule for a few hours a week when they are treated with respect and a kind of worship by burly men. Indeed, the same men who jeer at these drags during the day gather here at night to leer at them and fantasize about slipping it up them while fingering bra clad male nipples and taped down cocks only partially hidden by lacy panties. I'm not sure where my appeal fits into these fantasies but I've seldom gone home without a handsome man, most of them who are into playing Bottom. It's also a factual, rather than a racist, statement that of the five or six men I've slept with from here, all of them have been named Jose. Not being one to remember names, I'm greatly relieved to be able to whisper "Jose" into the ear of any old trick who wraps his arms around me.

I've always thought the goal of transvestites, as opposed to drag queens, is to attain a certain amount of "realness." My favorite transvestite friend, Roberta, is sitting pertly at the near bar waving to me as I come in. Now, Roberta's vision of realness is unique but to her this is what a proper lady looks like and, above all, Roberta is proper. Roberta has adopted a sort of spinster librarian look replete with a snug polyester blend pantsuit and big, ugly glasses. Her shoes are always practical in taupe with a low heel. "Honey," I say as I kiss her hello, "you look stunning tonight. That's a new doo you're sporting."

"Well, darlin'," she says wiping the pink smudge from my cheek, "my hair is one of my most fascinating assets. I looked in the mirror today and thought, this hair looks damaged and frizzy as a harlot's. Naturally, I was appalled having worked so hard on keeping myself up and still being such a young woman. So I thought a change was in order and I saw the cutest little girl on the street wearing her hair in a bun just like this. Do you really like it?"

Her hair being relatively short and frizzy, the bun looks like a wadded up nylon stuck to the back of her head but I have to admit it goes along with the librarian look. "Not only do I love it, but every man in this room is staring at you." And they were.

"Oh, sweetheart," she said with another peck to my cheek, "you say the nicest things. I hope you noticed my new shoes which all but saved my life tonight. They have this real comfortable heel, and you know how my feet bother me. Well, tonight I was about a block from the club, minding my own business when these two ruffians started following me. Being a woman of the world, I can tell when trouble is on the way. I pretended not to notice but started walking a little faster. Sure enough, the next thing I hear is 'Hey, sister, let me smell your panties. Pussy, pussy, pussy, pussy, pussy.' These boys obviously did not know that I was something of a track star in my school days and off I took with my sensible little heels clicking along like the Metroliner."

"You're a brave bitch, Roberta."

"That's right, honey, and if I can't run I fight. Say, let's get ourselves together a fag street gang and go over to Paramus and beat up some straighties. I'll give those shopping mall fashion disasters something to worry about." Her little push-up bra titties are waving in the air she's so proud. And she is brave, all these drags and TVs are brave because they don't have anywhere else to come but this ruined block late at night and they come. Men all through Brooklyn and Queens and the Bronx and Long Island and Jersey are slipping into pantyhose and sequined halter tops and heading for the city for this one night of being themselves and they don't care who the fuck they have to fight to get here. Some weekends you'll come in here and there'll be a queen strutting around with a black eye that can't be covered by the makeup or even an arm in a sling made of a bright patterned fabric. Those queens are treated with respect because they're saying they don't care what the world does to them, they won't change.

"Not to bring up a sore subject, honey, but I heard there was quite a little show over at Signal the other night," Roberta continues, suddenly intimate and quiet. "I ran into the sawed-off little queen you work for and she said things were over. And I do mean totally over."

"Yeah, what else did the queen of downtown tell you? Did she mention her latest magazine spread where her ass looked as wide as Pennsylvania?"

"Oooh, she didn't have to tell me about that, baby. I saw it with my own sparkling eyes. And in an architecture magazine, yet. I thought it was an article on the Hoover Dam when I got a gander of her backside. She did mention she has a new boyfriend, though. Some hot little Italian stallion performance artist she discovered. The show! The show!" Roberta squeals as she leaps up pushing through the crowd to get close to the stage. I need more beer to picture Ronny and the Dietro brother curled up at home in their love nest.

The show here is mostly incomprehensible to me because of the references to famous Puerto Rican goddesses of the screen and the wavery songs that the divas lipsynch to. The entire dance floor is cleared and used as performing area for the elaborately bowed and flounced drags to shimmy about on. The first time I came here I thought that this dance floor must have been the one they used to shoot "Saturday Night Fever" on because of the corny flashing lights in the raised floor. There is always a Mistress of Ceremonies that controls the seemingly endless parade of beauties with a costume change between every appearance. It's not that I don't like or appreciate the Zip-Zip show but it is much harder to meet guys once it begins because of the total concentration the butches afford it, often strutting onstage to stuff dollars in the simulated cleavage of favorites. Their big hands slide slow down the padded bras, shoving the bills far in and giving the shaved tits a good feel.

I have to admit the Mistress of Ceremonies has outdone herself tonight with a costume which makes her appear headless. Her head has been hidden by big, puffy fake shoulders and she teeters about, at least 6'3" in heels. Whether this is an in-joke or a bit of bizarreness, the audience screams with disbelief as she zooms down the length of the stage to sit on men's laps or point her glamour length nails at a rival in the audience. Everyone is cheering by the time she starts in on her song with the mike poking up into the air where her head should be. She's padded her hips and forms a perfect sequined hourglass, tottering from side to side nearly falling off the ledge. The song has been remixed so that the chorus, long and plaintive, comes again and again. I don't understand the words so I make up the meaning, a dark man in a dark suit silhouetted against the moonlit bay left her, knowing that she belonged to someone else, that she could never lie in his arms and say she wouldn't leave once the dawn came.

One man isn't paying any attention to her, obviously looking for something else. I circle him after getting a beer. Just my type, he has a sturdy compact body with a BMW T-shirt clinging to the slight curve of his stomach and tits. His face is magnificent with the ubiquitous close cropped moustache and long arched nose below black eyes and short, dark

84

hair. I get so close that I think I can smell the perfume of his brown, sleek skin sweating through his shorts.

I'd like to watch him wash that solid, thick stomach, letting his hand wander down to the jet black curls under his navel, the soapy hair getting whiter and whiter.

He meets my eyes immediately, without reservation. There is no need for small talk with this kind of man. Instead, he moves behind me and I feel his hand outlining my ass and his hip rolling up against mine. The show and the club are gone now while we make out. His is a face, a body, I can never believe when I touch them, too beautiful to be real. I don't think that most of the clientele here approves of this behavior but are too busy with the show to stare much. Having asked my name, he responds with his own, Juan. Uh oh.

"Leave with me, Juan," I urge almost immediately.

"Too early, man."

"Leave with me, Juan. Now." I stare my green eyes into his black ones until his tongue finds my mouth again.

The cabs zoom by outside swerving to the sides of the avenues to pick up fares ready to abandon the search for the night. As our cab swings over to Broadway and downtown, Juan and I feel each other's bodies and faces and crouch low in the seat fastened together. I never believed that people did this in the back of cabs like they do in movies about New York. But here I am gliding down Broadway with the hard body of a young man pushing against my face. Your eyes are pulling me in and down. You have a face that I will remember even though we will never speak again. You will be placed in a compartment of my brain which contains the features of all the men I might have wanted to take me and keep me and not leave right away. I can think of an innumerable number of things my tongue could do to your body, that your body could do to mine.

Later, as we float upwards in the elevator I'm tearing at his face and his neck and I want this man for more than a few moments and I want to give him what he will take. It seems like the elevator has forgotten where to go as the ride stretches longer and longer without end. This elevator has become a room and it's forgotten which way to go, it may slip diagonally or horizontally through the brick of the building, never opening, never letting us go. When the door finally slides silently open the lights of the hall are flickering, acidly, the paint too white and the pattern of the carpet threatening to contort into hallucination at any moment. I always keep my keys above the door so I don't lose them while I'm out and reaching up for them I feel my ribs separating and rippling.

"Do you want a drink," I ask, suddenly formal now in this familiar environment.

"No."

"Well, come in at least. Don't stay in the hallway. Come here to me."

His short body is very still in the entryway and his voice is low, "What do you think I'm going to do?"

"You're going to kiss me," I say as I head back towards him.

"Keep the fuck away from me, faggot."

Things are frozen and quiet here in the night as I sink down on a chair pointed towards the abyss between me and the lights of the skyline. His voice is so still I'm not sure if he's really still speaking and if I turn around maybe I'll find myself here alone, "Do you think I'm just giving it away? I hate the color of your skin, all white with those slapped up red cheeks. I hate the smell of you and your clean, clean breath. I hate the look of you in your pink little room with these prissy paintings."

"Then why are you here, my sexy monster?" I say turning to find him in the same place.

"I'm not your fucking anything, faggot. I'm not nothing but your fucking trouble," and he's close now so I smell him again and want him again and want to cry and sleep. His black eyes are lifeless, the eyes of a dead animal. "I want some payment for this little trip. You come in with your white boy attitude and pull me out before the show ends and I want some pay."

I pull my wallet out and start tossing the money and cards at his chest one at time until the contents are scattered around his hightop tennis shoes. "That's not what I want, asshole," he growls and I turn my head up to him like Tom does to me at The Hook. My mind is draining out slowly, the force of the suction drawing down my personality like the little tornadoes that form in the bathwater after the stopper is pulled. His voice is still low, sounds almost tender, "Give me that ring you got on. Let me see that fucking ring."

"No." The ring that belonged to my grandmother that never leaves my finger. The wedding ring of my grandmother made of tri-colored gold hammered into grape leaves and vines. Black Hills gold. The ring that circled her finger all those years. The only touch of my family I allow. The memory of her that is with me even as I run my hand over the cock of a man. "No."

"Don't tell me no you fucker. Don't you never tell me no," he screams as his hand slaps me back in the chair and off it. His voice is as shrill now as it was soft, as ugly as I could have asked for, "Give me that ring or you're dead meat you fat piece of shit."

A wail starts pulling my stomach and out my mouth as my arm extends back and up with the hand rigid like a claw. My grandmother's ring slides from my finger as his foot impacts my face and chest over and over. My body is like the brother's in Dietro, opening to the blows, accepting each reward with gratitude. You don't know how far down I can go...

SATURDAY

I lie rigid on the bed. Naked arms extend to the sides and, now, grasp the sheet. Pale white outline on white sheet in silent room with the hours slipping past unseen. White pale body disrupted by black hair splayed down, down over face and around cock throbbing vicious red. Purplish black circles and paisleys swirling patterns of abuse along stomach, chest, face, testifying to violence. Another hour joins the count. I rouse slightly only to swallow two more chalky yellow white pills scattered on carpet and grab for the tiny dark brown bottle sitting ready on the nightstand. Thin muscles of this thin arm work in opposition to the black capped bottle. Eventually free and fill the room. Sour, sour perfume. Chest bulges, greedy, filling with poisonous air and the strained wheeze comes out. Barely manage to restopper the brew and back, return the bottle to its post.

Now my hands begin to rove again, divorced from mind while pulling and tweaking and slapping white flesh until red, rosy handprints cover its surface.

Movements move, ever lower. Now to begin, once again. Cock begins heavy, heaving ritual again, draining all resistance from the body, wringing forth the form of drizzling, thin white liquid. A few slight, shudders and we return. Room in stillness and body immobile again on rocky hard slabs. Each time. Process repeats. Process repeats. Form more brittle, glasslike until now it seems even weak shafts of daylight creeping past me may be enough, yes, nearly enough to shatter. Room unnaturally neat and tidy. I expect a maid to slip in quietly, refold the blue jacket, smooth the khaki pants and gently slip out once again. But no one comes. No one calls. And sleep continues undisturbed.

I feel the breath move into me like liquid pouring down through nostrils and into my chest, porous, full. The acrid aroma of my body's hair and secretions and skin mix with the chemical rush of popper heaven. Now I do not think. Now I do not feel. Now I am separate from the rest. At peace, a frozen peace.

How long will this sleep continue and will it be restorative and what will finally rouse me? Distant sounds leak past barricades from time to time; civilized tones of old lady televisions broadcasting Chopin and the pirouettes of one more ballet, shouts and thud, thud, thud of balls in the court below, mysterious scrapes of lame feet from apartment above and constant squealing traffic. But all noise is muffled here by thin sheets of glass. A uniform roar eventually accepted. Indeed, when one travels from these confines, the absence of sound at night prohibits sleep. One lies restless, wondering if screams or groans of passion might suddenly thunder across the prairie night. No noise disturbs my sleep. Sleep is more than a physical need, a falling away from the world, a suicide punctuated by life.

But yet, it follows. Logical. Necessary. To sleep in once great cities in 1989. Snow has melted from the city and residents confront spring bringing not life this year, not hope but only more of the same death. The central fact of this town. Physical death, certainly, but also the death of spirit, waning throughout a dreary decade until finally bitter winter killed it off. New York is finally dead. Art of the future. To sleep. Here where too precious for real artists to live, homeless are packed away, dirty cartons in abandoned factories or discarded on the streets. Urban education for urban guerrillas. As it continues, one notices fewer and fewer dim outlines on the streets. Finally, no one, nothing left but bedrooms of forbidding steel buildings occupied by sleepers, trying to forget they are New Yorkers.

In the kitchen, an occasional cockroach sticks its antennae through steel grates of steel sink to smell for debris. Nothing yet, nothing here. Porcelain kitchen, barren smell, no food prepared on the stove in many months. Refrigerator holds only plastic scents, Diet Coke, mustardy bottle, ice, tray after tray of ice. Yet it follows, humanized by cooking and no cook here. Kitchens never used but for the same meal night after night. Small man from a Chinese restaurant taps at door. Dishware plastic, but included and no water, no dirt, no wash. Clean. Remember, food touches countertops, touches ceramic dishes, touches silver and activates a kitchen demanding more. Actual preparation of food involving increasingly elaborate recipes. Finally entire days subsumed in shopping and dicing and washing and serving. The fear of people who own unused, howling kitchens. This kitchen gazes north at sharp crags and stone valleys of buildings full of workers. Through the motions, going through daily routines not realizing that to the south someone has withdrawn from life, from struggle into a separate world. Blinds drawn, always drawn, the usual call of daylight having lost its appeal. Workers running to Xerox, fight the boss and think of quitting. All within sight of cockroaches sitting in sterile kitchens admiring the hazy, unimportant view.

Darkness brings an insanity. Possible now. Just barely possible to wake for a few hours. The blinds no longer let in long light knives and without warning, he stands. Straight up. Abruptly from the bed but not move. Not yet move but the pain, the pain to rip and shatter. Maybe I've not been sleeping at all, just forcing my eyes shut long after the conscious mind awoke. Standing, not moving, looking down at the black and white body and the neat room and my eyes fully awake, empty of emotion. Blank. Long sweeps of my thin arm sufficient to destroy the maddening order of the room. Jacket, blue jacket tumbles floorward, arms crossing themselves with disinterest. Little stinky brown bottle slowly etches its contents into deep blue silk, eating in like gasoline into Styrofoam. Tortured garment. From across the city, another slowly nods, pushes greasy hair back up under a baseball cap. Yes, the way to wear it. Tortured, dirty, ripped beyond recognition. Yes, now we begin.

I will not look, how could I look to the mirrors that will reflect this horror in full, revealing my transformation from a human to a little less, a little less now than human. Must avoid that glassy torture while picking into bathroom to lean over the bowl, ready to discharge the contents of my body, of my mouth, of my ass, of my cock, of my eyes. But a moment's calm first, staring into the bowl at a tissue left floating like a lung on the slowly lapping water. Someone has taken out my lung, I do believe, removed my lung without permission and left it in the toidy, breathing steady, waiting for me to return. Gone now though with the first rush of black and red and tan from my stomach, filling the bowl with bile and blood. Flush and flush again but always more from another mysterious valve on my body. This hate roars liquid from my mouth, exploding too from my ass. My eyes too tired to weep more and my cock too used to emit the last deep yellow.

I will not clean this body but leave it as a testament. Offer it as low enough now for all takers, none rejected, none unfit to work as vultures for the last few scraps of meat. Walking carrion, I must go to the meat district before I miss my appointment. There's a tall, hairy man in white waiting for me there, wiping his gloves against his jacket, wondering where that last piece of meat is. Where that last side of beef is. His cock will swing wide in the loose bag of his pants when he finally hauls me up with those great heaving shoulders, sweating with the effort and coating the fur of his back with a fine, salty mist. Everything will shoot past, child on a swing, and up I go for the last ride, the last arcing trip to the shiny resting point. On the hook at last, hanging heavy as he pats me down, looking satisfied, rubbing his moist groin one last time before home to wife and child.

Familiar objects; long, beaten leather coat to sweep the path, jeans, heavy shoes all pulled on quickly over dirty skin and stinking hair. Keys and money discarded in favor of a black baseball cap and out. Slam through door and back to the streets of an ever darkening city. Lobby nearly deserted at this homely hour. People content in cozy apartments with the evening news beaming in human interest. The same stories night after night. More unpleasant, highly visible issues somehow missing. Cramped apartments, viewers enthralled, cooing over armless pianists and rescue dogs and retarded teachers and exploring canoers and Long Island gypsies and disco grannies. Coos grand enough to shiver the building, almost collapsing the old structure as I gain the strength to enter the evening and head west to the river.

Not quite empty, not quite deserted because of you. You stinking little brown man. Tonight, Franky, tonight of all nights you have the gall to stare at me, to notice me and my shards of clothes rattling through the lobby. Tonight, you stare not only at me but at my eyes with a look that says you knew it all along. Then you'd better tell me what you know, what you see. "What the fuck are you looking at, Franky?" No response but no backing off. "Like what you see, big man? Maybe you'd like a taste, a sniff. Not so different from some pickly briny fish. Just give it to me. No big deal. Just slip it in, baby, I won't even notice. I'm just a big fucking hole waiting for you, Franky. And I know it's what you want. Now I'm just right for you, daddy man, just right to get tossed in your car for a little trip to Queens. Not too busy now, let's just leave. Wanna slap me around a little bit, show me that bedroom? Or are you afraid to get red all over those pretty white walls? Don't worry about me, I ain't got no red left inside, no pink, no white, no brown. Dry as a bone and twice as tasty inside. Why don't you just fry me up for dinner tonight, Franky boy? Oh, I'm a tender piece of meat after you beat me a little. How about it, Franky, wanna go out to Queens and tenderize me?" No response, no reaction, just the blank brown eyes thinking about a room already full, full to the brim with boys like me.

Lurching, plodding figure passes stone park. Same, just the same, as so many nights. Tonight no word from dark dealers around the dry fountain. This night the potted rats cast eyes guiltily down as my figure passes over them. This night buzzing fluorescent lights cast a long shadow stretching down Waverly to the fork where it meets Christopher Street. An itinerary. Unconsciously set for the evening. Towards the water always and then turn, sharp turn. Path set and will be followed this every night. Low glare at Stonewall but none of the original anger, no queens, only levis and muscle. Hungry men in the light, silhouetted. Lean, starving outlines moving indecisively. I begin. Past the men, leering at each. Rubbing a welcome. Quite a sight, the long coated man stumbling where once walked regally. No welcome returned by this lot. Rumbling asses in Levi's turn quickly back to fern bars and talk of the island and forget someone has slipped. Someone has finally fallen. On to more desperate territory.

No activity at the bookstore. Unusual. Only smell and empty booths and me, the man in long leather sunk down. Sunk down where never before. Hard cold floor alive with non-human activity. I barely notice the gentle antennae tickling, waving welcome across my hand, quickly over my body. Perky Peanut's salute unnoticed by unnoticing eyes focused on long lines of empty booths. No click of the turnstile. No whisper of the screens. Only smell. Sour reminder of other evenings when crowds passed and felt and sampled the flesh. No live men only ghosts of old tricks, saying goodbye. Tricks from across a country of use, West Hollywood, Chicago's Rush and downtown New York. Slap, slap go weightless feet past a crumpled boy. Now, we begin to lose sight of him, lose him, the tangle of streets providing ever more fleeting glimpses. Dimmer and dimmer around the circuit of booths and in to explore left treasures; wrinkled condoms, smeared screens and scratchy numbers for shit slave, hungry ass, fist buddy, pussy boy, whip master, head cheese, dripping pits, j/o, boot licker, do what you want, wrestling partner, v/a, loose throat, greasy hole, fat cock, medical scene, bubble ass, piss drinker, fuck hole sucker, daddy, son, rubber freak, slave. Do what you want.

Dark in here and I don't know the hour, don't care about the passing time. May be day outside of these tinny walls. But no one comes. No one tonight. Only the chatter of the queens arranging the porno videos out front. They didn't recognize me as I came in, didn't look alarmed. Seen too many already. One a night, I suppose. At least one that inches to the turnstile, imploring looks, no money but please, please just let me escape. Another rag bag needs the dark in back and they allow it, allow another casualty of war to pass into the stinking sanctuary for free. The costs of this war are escalating. I can feel the half dead moving outside these walls in dark or light, still moving but no longer feeling.

Too quiet here. Too contemplative and I seek noise. Blind noise ripping out thought and speech. Roar of traffic better for all. Short path down Christopher. No signals so walk. Just walk and see. Yet, they slow. Cars moving slower and finally stopping to let my plodding figure pass unharmed to other side. Other side where lights swing round for another look. Water laps to blend with squealing tires and Puerto Rican girls whispering, pointing, clicking on. Piers frighten me tonight. Unclear activity, mysterious movement out to sea. Hazy pier arms extending to water. Men lounge on cement walls with one lone boy turning and turning at the end. Dancing, turning at the end of the pier as all the others watch. Can't hear the music but must be, must be some impetus to turn and wheel and fly all alone. At the end of the long pier.

I stay by the road, safer. Cars of all shapes but the tinted windows...want those. Yearn for tinted windows and fat arms and pushing, forcing hands. Men from hellish lives here to use. One another. Use and forget. And so I walk to each, fear suddenly gone, unimportant. Stare through the glass to frightened faces. Cruel faces. Stare at the eyes. Unacceptable gesture. Taboo. Correct is glance to eyes, uninterested, glance down, away. But I meet and lock eyes and not away but closer, rubbing, leaning. Men embarrassed, slightly angry. I tap at the window, no reply. Tap harder, no reply. Knock hard and open looks of fear cross their faces as the motor purrs to action and the car glides away. Red taillights winking. Down the line. Each the same. No reply. Why are they afraid of me now when used to want, used to want these blue eyes rolling with pleasure? Different now.

End of the line finally. Must reach the end eventually and at the end of the line is a structure. A building by the water housing much but supposedly housing only salt. Salt to scatter on icy winter roads but not winter now and more than salt. Slip through doors to the mountainous terrain, moonscape of salt dunes a dirty grayish white. Small fires burn and encampments perch between dunes and beside walls further along. Skyline vistas glimpsed through tin-less holes gaping at all levels letting all in. Salty rats and salty dogs and dusty, salty children wandering or resting or simply staring straight ahead. Always a film floats through the air to obscure half-lit corners and deep valleys where sex happens. Barren setting. Stage set. Unreal at night, worse during day. Where parents have sent them, to see them. Dead on the evening news. Not there even. Dead but seen nowhere. Not these salty children. Only innocent victims allowed for the general readership.

These are my children and here we'll make our humble home. They go out and work while I tidy up salty house, bake salty bread for their hungry, greedy stomachs. No clean water so rub their stiff clothes with the grains, cleanse the stained, ripped jeans and smell the sweat of their thick, hairy thighs. Young sweat so sweet I don't mind. Don't mind attending my many children. But their eyes are gone, too. Blank like mine, runs in the family. Stumble back through doors with another layer of soot to cover the jacket's caked filth.

Now truly at an impasse. Only blank walls or buzzing highway. Bloody streets of meat across the nine lanes, waiting. My head turns to cars, head turns to water, head turns to salt, head turns to sky, head turns to ground, head turns to Meat. Now to navigate. More dangerous here at this end of the walk. No signs, no witnesses. Hit and run. A game for some cruel men. Accelerate and blue license plate last thing seen. Creep to triangular dividers, barely in time for the next rush in the stream. Wait, creep and finally bolt one last time past wide lanes and blaring horns of enemies. Not to safety but to familiar quiet, waiting hook. Shoulders of the jacket lower slightly at entering home ground. And quiet now. And quiet now and home and safe and so far gone but not much further to go.

Streets smear underfoot leaving trails of slow prints. Dragging in the same direction, leaving a map that will dissolve when rain comes. Tonight a map is left for other brothers to follow through steel woods, past the wilderness and into empty street. Walls of metal, protecting, hiding. Only a dim beat, beat, beat echoes against concrete and steel frames. Sign to follow. I know where leads, always knew, had to and the beat continues faintly. Almost there. Till in the distance the glow begins. Red door. Wander past abandoned warehouses till finding the red door. Once you wake a room, it stays alive. It beats like murderer's basement. Tells you that it waits. Impatient. Open Me. See Me. Know Me. Give It To Me. Lurch on to the sound, the signal, the alive basement and room and stairway and red door always searched for finally found.

And now this dim black coated figure leans against a dim black painted building and listens. To the beat. As it continues. I pull weakly at the door, badly chained. This the place and here now and home and I must enter my home to finally have some rest. Holes in floor. Faggat. No trespassing. Pull again and again at chained door first with arms, then with whole body. Throwing body back, convulsing against chains. Door slamming against restraint harder and harder. Chains, chains wrapped around this door, around me and beginning to cut into the soft unprotected palms of this weak body. Links of chain pressing into the flesh, not content with outer surfaces they must move deeper yet. Silent. Blood starts to flow from my steel ripped fingers and tattered cheek but, again, body throws back with all its thin might. First crack of wood is heard. Beat grows stronger as chains rasp against rotting doors. Organ in the chapel breathes tentatively, trying first one slow scale and then whistling notes of a prelude. Slam and slam again goes my thin, separate body. Force gathering beyond its weight. Another crack and I fly backwards, chains rattling around my thick shoes and dirty jeans. An open portal. And now it begins.

Liquid black through the opening. Odors compressed, distilled now flow free. And doors creak open to welcome. Home now and safe and we will never leave again. Lever leather thin body up. Vertical, it teeters forward. Close and breathe in the air. To the dark red door and stop at threshold, pause and then slowly sucked in, to the bottom, at the bottom. No lower. Dim figure fades into interior, soon lost to sight, soon lost to all. Spiral back to long view of rickety streets in far West Manhattan, waves lapping at the edge. Welcoming him home.

SUNDAY

I'm still alive this morning. This afternoon. This evening. Not supposed to be but still alive so I lie in the water as it laps against the yellow soap rings in the bath, washes my body slowly. What a sight this body is. Not me. Bruises turning bluer by the moment, vicious rips in the skin, swelling on the face and around the skinned knee. Peaceful here at the improvised shore as I clean this body carefully, methodically. Wash the heavy grease from my hair. Again and again I lather, urging the grease to let go its hold. Finally, the black hair sweeps into a curve along my battered cheek and lies gracefully in place, clean. The plastic shower curtain hangs limp beside me, whitish mold creeping up its plastic blue length in the shapes of wizened faces and clouds and animals that stare back at me.

The surface destruction of my body doesn't bother me so much. Deep inside, though, there have been changes. There is no pain through my abdomen, chest, limbs. Only a deep, insistent throbbing in my left temple belies a pressure below. There is no pain but an awareness of the tender organs, of the liver not to be touched for fear of bursting, of the lungs full of air but also other things, of the kidneys hard against the ribs, of my throat drawing for liquid and of my ass stretched and slack and bleeding slightly. Even these don't worry me as much as my head, specifically my brain which does not feel at all and is, in fact, numb. I can think but I cannot feel and it's a physical destruction of something deep inside my brain that makes it so. How much can the body heal and when does it stop being immortal and what is an injury and what is a handicap? Something has passed but the price of the fever has been high and the passing brings only an accounting of damage, not relief.

I may have died and this is one of those out-of-body experiences one hears about in trashy tabloids. This may be the result of death, everything's the same but more boring, more sedate. One wouldn't mind if it was possible to at least take that wild tunnel trip with a bright light at the end. But no, only the dingy bathroom with the ancient tub, finish gouged in spots and smelling of cleanser from long ago. Staring at the bare lightbulb is soothing, though. If I stare at it long enough I turn blind and all the objects on the periphery of my vision quiver, disappear. After a few minutes, my eyes adjust and I can see the filament burning within the vacuum bulb, burning and searing, ready to break with a sizzle and a snapping sound. The filament goes on and on burning itself, wanting to die.

No one in my small family has ever died, excepting a grandfather I never knew. None of my friends has ever died. None of my acquaintances has ever died. None of my colleagues has ever died. I've never even known anyone seriously ill. I have never been touched by the death that runs so readily through this city. Fascination with death comes from it always swirling close around one's head but never touching directly. Very likely death becomes mundane with repetition, numbing, anything but a romantic vision, producing only anger and pragmatism. Never having known death, I can survey this body in the splashing water and see the beauty of its white curves marred by dark purple and red. The bruises don't look so much different from lesions and I can easily imagine a different kind of quiet violence transforming this body in the same way. I can still look at this death and admire it because I have never known it but may soon.

The water finally drains leaving a wrinkled, little body. Although it's stupid, sometimes after long days and nights in the city one wants to put on white clothes. Not ubiquitous black. Pull on layers of starched white and soft white and long white as in a hospital or a country house or an ad. And that's what I feel I must do now, cover my bruises in healing layers of white clothes and then sit very still in some clean corner and wait. Wait and decide. Tonight in New York there's a faint breeze blowing the dirt around and I've opened the windows so that the air in the room moves slowly past me. The courtyard of the building emits little peeps of noise from other apartments that barely make it past the roar of traffic. The fat man across the way is cooking again, making what he makes every night for his dinner, fried hamburgers and fried onions and probably a tater tot casserole or some other culinary delight as a side dish. I'm still and little as he whirs and puffs about his kitchen, intent on the food that he can never quite wait for, just a bite to taste. In my kitchen lies a pizza box, a dirty plate and several Diet Coke cans.

Decisions can never be made inside. There's no avoiding the streets below any longer. A very old lady rides down on the elevator with me. She lives on my floor but is next to blind and deaf so she never recognizes me as a neighbor. She peers at my face, the wrinkly folds of skins bunched up around her eyes, turning her head from side to side trying to get a better view. When she has decided that I must be someone she's met before she nods her white bun of hair and tells me the story she tells me at least once a week, "I'm one hundred and one years old. No, I'm ninety-one years old. I've lived in this place for fifty-five years. This was a good building once, but now...This place is a second-rate house. They won't fix my walls, I want them to fix my walls. I moved in before the elevators worked. My husband is dead. I'm all alone. I want them to fix my walls. What number is that? I can't read the numbers on this elevator, fifty-five years and now they change the buttons and I can't read it. I walked the stairs up here before they even put in these elevators, oh, they were pretty then, men with white gloves in the elevators. Not now, no way. Oh, they're horrible. They won't fix my walls." Mrs. Lubash is right, they won't fix her walls and they should. Her palatial apartment towers over the city but the walls are crumbling from water damage, covered in plastic stuck to them with thumbtacks and straight pins. They'll never fix Mrs. Lubash's walls. It's cheaper to pay the lawyers to stall until she finally croaks.

All the old ladies are out this evening. Going to the opera or to Gristedes or walking their dirty little dogs. They've convened on the sofas in the lobby to socialize for a while and only give me a quick look as I walk past. Either Franky hasn't told them about last night or the gossip network hasn't gotten it around to everyone yet. He might not tell them because maybe what I said was true. I wonder if he's thinking about it tonight as he sits at home in his undershorts running his hands over his big belly. Outside the city doesn't seem new to me. New York is an ancient city in my eyes tonight with feuds never settled, corruption never rooted out, art never new and people always old. And it's not New York, it's Manhattan. Let's get that straight. This island, this borough, has nothing to do with Queens or Brooklyn or the Bronx or Staten Island. It's separate and for all the politically correct posturing it will remain separate, sneering at all the other poor cousins until the end. What do we know of even Brooklyn? It may as well be the Arctic Circle. I have no desire to go there or know about it or be a part of it and anyone who says they do is lying. This is Manhattan and it's old and dead but decisions must still be made here.

I must decide on these streets tonight what to do because all those small, theatrical events have finally added up. A change wasn't pointed out for me but the need was. I have no more money, no friends, no job and no interests. At that point one must either decide to throw the last scraps of life away in a glorious final burn or find a way out.

Tonight's walk has no itinerary. I move instinctually in the same direction as always but for different reasons. I look in front of me, eyes fixed and step intently down Christopher to the water. Everyone's resting today and Christopher is nearly deserted as is the broken highway at its end. I cross easily to the abandoned piers, looking so sad with only a few scattered figures meandering about, not sure if they even want any more sex this weekend. Usually, I stay strictly to the area the cars use to circle but tonight I'm drawn out onto one of the piers themselves. This one has been feebly chained shut and then quickly ripped back open by the men. The ugly orange sign tells patrons the pier is dangerous, as if they couldn't tell by the gaping holes in the wood through which you can see the water splashing. I pick my way over the rotting wood and candy bar wrappers and rubbers to the end. No one else is here, tonight. Only things far in the distance look beautiful, the woods on the Jersey side, the new buildings downtown, the little houses of the Village. Up close, however, the water still stinks and the long tail of a rat sticks out from a crack, twitching, twitching.

Where is everyone tonight? Manhattan has people

stuffed into every available corner and tonight there is no one, as if the ground cracked open and swallowed them all. Maybe they'd finally had enough and left. Evacuated. Big grey buses, all packed with New Yorkers heading out. Each group has its separate bus with the queens having the best ones, festooned with banners and glamour magazines. The Yuppies sit very still in their bus, the women have on little suits with ribbon ties and tennis shoes, the men try to relax in their velour running suits, but everyone is tense as they are out of jobs and without jobs the Yups have no identity, no purpose. They sneer as the flotilla of queen buses pulls past, hooting, mooning through the windows. I've missed the buses, though, so I'll stay here because the city is only part of the problem in my case.

It's time to go back to the dark apartment, to the TV and the old ladies. But rather than continuing East along Christopher, when I reach Seventh Avenue, I turn uptown. Up Seventh past the sleazy street cafes for gay tourists and the Pleasure Chest and five restaurants all called Szechuan Balcony. Looking up the avenues from the Village one is always caught by the overpowering stone canyons of Midtown in the distance. Nothing could change those cold concrete forms. The only thing to do is to empty them, drain the people from their bases and let them sit, ruins. There is an echo in the canyon tonight, a ringing of voices which dribbles down to me from around Fourteenth Street. Vague movement and rhythmic voices draw me on.

A group of protestors, gay men and lesbians, boils up out of a brick building and into the streets. More and more push through the door, in couples, singly and in knots of friends. Their chants are simple, two line verses about AIDS and homophobia. The stereotypical images of AIDS are not in this street, in their ranks. Either the truly ill do not protest or they are just looking very good, basking in the excitement of the activity. Some are thin, slightly pale but all walk sturdily and reveal their bodies rather than hiding them under layers of clothes. One man is covered with raspberry purplish lesions but actually wears them as a badge of courage with a tanktop and short shorts barely covering his strong limbs so that the spots flash on the tan flesh, no shame. From the distance of the papers and TV one sees only wasting men, always white and certainly never a woman, lying in hospital beds with snakes and webs of tubes impaling their flesh. Those men always have moustaches and short hair as if to attest to their fault in leading the "clone" lifestyle which melded financial power and sexual abandon. I don't see those men here but their images continue to flash in my mind with the shrill media voices reprimanding, "You see. You see what happens."

They're laughing and moving quickly. The grand marshall of the impromptu parade is a queen on roller skates with a white lacy gown, cinched tight around her waist and she's in the middle of the street skating a tight circle. "The fairy godmother says fight back," she wails in a shrill Southern accent. She's something of an institution and I recognize her wheeled wonder from descriptions of the grand old days of New York nightlife when Truman Capote would snort coke at Studio 54 surrounded by Lee Radziwell and Barbara Walters and C.Z. Guest and Liza Minnelli and Liz Taylor and Ultra Violet and boys from the sailor bars. Grand old days when Mapplethorpe would fist investment bankers and Malcolm Forbes and Ed Koch and Virgil Thomson and Dick Cavett and Stephen Sondheim and Kenneth and Steve Rubell and the mustached Fire Island set in the balcony of The Saint. Cum and coke and old movie theatres painted black while they fucked and danced till morning waiting for Grace Jones or some other disco diva to take the stage and then on to the baths for more. Well, this is one historic figure who's very much alive and gay, motoring around the avenue, skirt flying up and her glittery wand blessing all who pass. She does a little of the hokey-pokey and then swings on to new territory with a battle cry.

What a sight I am with my puffy blue bruises and a Band-Aid pasted over the cut below my eye. Yet I approach a beautiful man to ask what's going on. Apparently a woman died last night after a visit to the emergency room of a nearby hospital and the community has reports that the death was related to a beating by a security guard there. The woman had been raped and beaten and when her lover took her to the hospital, the homophobic reaction of the guards had been immediate and violent, beating both of them as they held hands. I can see that image so clearly in my mind that I don't think it'll ever go away, that image is grinding into my brain here on the street as the archetype of hate, of blind stupid hatred that's killing this city.

Inexplicably, I'm starting to cry here on Seventh Avenue with gay men and lesbians dressed in white and black T-shirts and torn jeans and big black shoes pouring past me, screaming. Here on this exposed strip of asphalt I've begun to weep about two women I don't know who were eaten by the hatred of this city like so many others. Fortunately, the man who told me the story stays alongside of me and holds my hand lightly, nonsexually, comforting and constantly talking. Jamison is his name, but he goes by Jim and his long, brownish red hair goes along with the WASPy name and the craggy Irish features. Irish faces absorb everything around them, tragedy, everyday happiness, harsh wind, sun, sex, religion. They soak in their environment calmly, a permanent blush appearing on them revealing their passage through life. Jamison too wears the uniform of baggy, old jeans and a white shirt which reveals a defined body. Nothing is more satisfying than the feel of a man's hard hand, soft in one's own. You forget wanting this, wanting to be in a sea of one's own. Not a secret society.

He tells me I've cried enough, stop crying and come along to the protest he says as we follow the crowd across Seventh Avenue. We cross slowly, single file to bring traffic to a halt for a few minutes. Drivers are either angry and try to inch through the line or completely ignore the situation as a normal New York traffic problem. One asshole starts bumping his pickup slowly into people and within a minute he's rocking back and forth, almost tipping over, with the entire vehicle covered in pink triangle stickers. I can't stop looking at his scrawny face screaming that he'll kill us, that we're dead anyway and his features are so contorted with hate that I think blood might come squirting right out his nose and mouth and ears. We hold hands as we snake one by one onto the sidewalk on the east side of the avenue and to the hospital. Guards are quickly locking doors and making phone calls to the police as hundreds of kissing dykes and fags begin to march in a loose circle. Fifty or so demonstrators made it into the waiting room before it was locked and we can see them through a huge plate glass window as they take the floor, refusing to leave. Burly security guards, looking worried and annoyed, do nothing as the big statue of Jesus is fitted with a condom and lipstick kisses are planted on the glass.

The kiss-in has formed concretely outside as police cars begin to arrive. There are two circles moving in opposite directions, a kiss for each passing pair of lips. Some I particularly relish, but all are remarkably friendly and accepting. I recognize a famous writer and political activist I admire. How can a writer slashed again and again by the pain of death, who talks of losing a hundred friends, bear to look at the page, at those idiot words? His work as a writer, as an artist, recedes next to the actual pain and heroism of his own life. I wonder how he can even bear to sit down to write when his life shows how unimportant, even nonsensical, the plays and paintings and books and performance art and symphonies and ballets and concerts and photographs appear in these dark days. When I kiss him I look to his eyes and they look so much happier, so much more at home than in the photos of him at his plays.

The circle becomes a protective wall against the squalling bull horns and cops erecting blue wooden barricades around the perimeter of our group. They're pushing us back from the street, closer and closer to the cold stone front of the hospital. This hospital has always sickened me when I'd walk by and ambulances would arrive at the emergency entrance which is located right on Seventh Avenue. Bleeding, screaming people on stretchers are maneuvered through rush hours traffic with pedestrians cursing at them to get out of the way. Red tracks down Seventh from cars sloshing through blood and red footprints from shoes straying too close and red abstract splatters from another shattered body. The poor humanity of New York. The city must hire special blood washers, teams of them wrapped in protective gear, scrubbing the scarlet streets after another busy day.

The television cameras have arrived and are pushing demonstrators out of their way as the reporter looks uninterested, waiting for the on air cue. One fat, greasy man corseted into a blue suit takes notes and chews on a piece of pizza. Where's the action, he wonders. He's disappointed having hoped for a juicy story in time for the eleven o'clock news. His shiny, red lips pucker up in disgust at the fags and lesbos he has to cover and then they're not even violent. There's hope, though, because he sees a few cops that he knows are handy with the nightsticks, always good for a few sly clubs. He thinks back to his all-time favorite stories; the boiled girlfriend, the three chopped children, the dog molester, the black riot and, of course, the leper colonies on the Bayou. He smiles, throwing the pizza crust on the ground, belching and thinking, God, I love this city.

This is all happening too fast and starting to escalate and I don't know where I am or who I'm with. Too fast but invigorating and I have nothing to lose. A woman is circulating though the line asking people if they're planning to be arrested. She's continuing along towards me in a black and pink T-shirt and my mind is frantically wondering who I could count on to worry as I sat in jail. Who will care if two, three days later, forgotten, I'm still chatting with rapists and murderers and grand larceny suspects. I say yes, I may be arrested and she takes down my phone number and address and who she can call to notify them. I have no one to depend upon, no one who will pick up the phone late at night and, recognizing my name, be concerned. In my wallet is the number of the thin, blonde woman from Signal. This will be a good early test of friendship. I can imagine her forehead wrinkling slightly as she sits in bed surrounded by cats, remembers the name and nods as she talks.

All around me people are wearing shirts and pins and stickers and hats engraved with the slogans of revolution. The most famous one, the one I see everywhere is still the most moving, however. A pink triangle spiking upwards on a field of black with Silence=Death shouting out underneath in white letters. I'm thinking of these long days in silence, in my self-imposed silent room as the city thunders outside and the nights eventually turning silent also. Nights, once full of idle chatter, have become deadly still lately. No talk, no sigh. Only rushed, wrenching bodies stretching on to infinity. Not to know one another is to acknowledge a shame or a guilt or a mark of inferiority. And that silence of men touching men and names never known, words never shared seems not so far from the stony silence of governments and bigots. When I glided those wet, greasy streets so still was there really no word to say to hungry prostitutes, nothing to discuss with men who could have abated my loneliness? Are all of my words gone?

Cops, nearing hysteria, are closing the allowed space. Their overly meaty, flushed faces are pinching, the eyes flat and blank. Soon their faces will go absolutely slack as they raise nightsticks and give way to the mindless violence which is their sex, their release. Who chooses to be a cop? Not the civic minded or the intellectual or the noble or the brave. No, killers and cruel hearted morons take up the blue uniform and hide their sadism behind a silver badge that gives them almost unlimited rights to people's lives and bodies. The line is being pushed tighter and tighter against the picture window of the waiting room. We're so tight up against the wall that the concentric circles are grinding up against one another like too tightened cogs. I no longer try to move down to the next partner but continue to kiss the young man across from me. He's my height, black with flattop hair and a curving, muscular body. I feel his chest against mine and he giggles through his short beard as we occasionally stop for breath or to chant. His name is Wayne. Packed in around us are other couples and trios of short haired dykes and long haired fags and long haired dykes and short haired fags, all tossed together in every possible combination. We start a new chant, "We'll never be silent again. ACT UP! We'll never be silent again." When our small area tires of it, we rest for a moment and I hear it echoing back from the brick walls of Seventh Avenue like the song of some grand choir.

Wayne's touching my battered face, the cut under my eye and I don't like it at first. It's embarrassing and I think it'll make me cry again but then I wonder if he thinks they're lesions rather than bruises. I don't tell him that they came from a man who kicked me and stole from me but let him think what he wants because now I want them to be badges of honor, like the drag queens at Zip-Zip have. Now that his finger traces the spots on my forearm, it doesn't matter where these marks came from, because all suffering is equal. Most people who get hurt don't deserve it and I didn't and those two women beat at the hospital didn't and the man who shows off his lesions didn't and all the dead, all the thousands and thousands of dead, who should be with us now, didn't deserve it either. We're all innocent.

They're warning everyone who stays that we'll be arrested. I ask Wayne whether he wants to stay and he kisses me some more. They're pushing still harder, trying to force people out and I can hear the popping crashing sound of the window as it shatters inward from the pressure. We're still kissing, this young man and I, when two cops push us over on our sides onto the concrete. Expecting the cold slap of handcuffs, I find disconcerting the cinching of plastic garbage ties around our wrists. They think of us as bags of garbage, toxic garbage to be guardedly handled by gloved hands. They'll wash their hands as soon as possible, these cops, wash them and rinse them with bleach after they take off their tight rubber gloves. I'm dragged in great jolts by the sweating, swearing cop and all the time I hear strangers cheering and yelling that they love me as Wayne and I are hauled towards the paddy wagon.

It's rather like going camping, getting loaded into a paddy wagon. All the kids are crowded into the back, joking or griping about having to piss or asking, "When will we be there?" Mom and Dad are up front, presumably doing unnecessary little chores, wasting time, checking maps or filling out arrest receipts. Inside the back of the car, everyone's happy and singing as loud as possible to annoy the parents.

Jamison is in the back grinning and Wayne is leaning his head on me, singing as we get ready to drive off. They haul in a big, beautiful dyke and she squeezes next to me, "Scoot over, honey, it's time for sister to go to jail. God bless our gay lives."

Amen.

BOOKS AVAILABLE FROM AMETHYST PRESS

IDOLS
By Dennis Cooper $8.95

BEDROOMS HAVE WINDOWS
By Kevin Killian $8.95

HORSE
By Bo Huston $8.95

MUSIC I NEVER DREAMED OF
By John Gilgun $8.95

THE BLACK MARBLE POOL
By Stan Leventhal $8.95

THE BURIED BODY
By Mark Ameen $10.95

THIS EVERY NIGHT
By Patrick Moore $8.95